A GRINGO WITH SOME

"What is your business here?" Reyas demanded.

"My own."

"Well, Slocum, you rode into my land uninvited. You take up with a lovely widow and you say you are here on your own business."

"Gawdamn, I looked on the map. Said this was Mexico. You, the *presidente*?"

"This is my land and these mountains are mine." Reyas stood upright and threw out his chest. "You're going to learn about my land. Th___ ___ in a cell."

"Reckon you can tell old C_____ vski that his chief scout is in your cell ___"

"Debrewski? Why is_____ list captain was not someone_____-to-face.

"Cap'n ain't s_____ boys roughing me up. I _____

"Slocum, _____ n going to personally cut your ___

"Don't worry _____ your own ass you better be saving." Slocum _____ in the stirrup and swung up on the bay. "Nice m___ing you."

Reyas watched him ride down the road, doffing his hat to a woman. That clown better be Debrewski's man or he'd shred him like tobacco.

DON'T MISS THESE
ALL-ACTION WESTERN SERIES
FROM THE BERKLEY PUBLISHING GROUP

THE GUNSMITH by J. R. Roberts

Clint Adams was a legend among lawmen, outlaws, and ladies. They called him . . . the Gunsmith.

LONGARM by Tabor Evans

The popular long-running series about Deputy U.S. Marshal Long—his life, his loves, his fight for justice.

SLOCUM by Jake Logan

Today's longest-running action Western. John Slocum rides a deadly trail of hot blood and cold steel.

BUSHWHACKERS by B. J. Lanagan

An action-packed series by the creators of Longarm! The rousing adventures of the most brutal gang of cutthroats ever assembled—Quantrill's Raiders.

DIAMONDBACK by Guy Brewer

Dex Yancey is Diamondback, a Southern gentleman turned con man when his brother cheats him out of the family fortune. Ladies love him. Gamblers hate him. But nobody pulls one over on Dex. . . .

WILDGUN by Jack Hanson

The blazing adventures of mountain man Will Barlow—from the creators of Longarm!

TEXAS TRACKER by Tom Calhoun

Meet J. T. Law: the most relentless—and dangerous—manhunter in all Texas. Where sheriffs and posses fail, he's the best man to bring in the most vicious outlaws—for a price.

JAKE LOGAN

SLOCUM DOWN MEXICO WAY

J

JOVE BOOKS, NEW YORK

SLOCUM DOWN MEXICO WAY

A Jove Book / published by arrangement with
the author

PRINTING HISTORY
Jove edition / February 2003

Copyright © 2003 by Penguin Putnam Inc.

Visit our website at
www.penguinputnam.com

ISBN: 0-515-13471-6

A JOVE BOOK®
Jove Books are published by The Berkley Publishing Group,
a division of Penguin Putnam Inc.,
375 Hudson Street, New York, New York 10014.
JOVE and the "J" design
are trademarks belonging to Penguin Putnam Inc.

PRINTED IN THE UNITED STATES OF AMERICA

10 9 8 7 6 5 4 3 2 1

Prologue

They rode in on jaded horses. Heads hung low, the animals snorted into the ground and their expired breath made the dust fly. The haggard riders formed a line, side by side before the rambling adobe house. Spur rowels clinked like silver spoons when the men dismounted heavily with sighs and groans.

A woman in her twenties came out on the porch. Her proud breasts pushed hard at the red silk material that encased them. Hands on her shapely hips, her narrowed eyes shining with black anger, she stood with her handmade boots set apart on the grit-worn wood floor. Her divided riding skirt was decorated down the sides with hand-hammered *conchos,* polished pesos that gleamed even in the shade.

"Did you find him?"

Sombrero off and covering his heart, her secondo Matamoris warily shook his head. "We never found him, señorita."

The quirt in her hand snaked out and she lashed it across the old man's face. Streaks of blood soon appeared on his white beard–stubbled cheek. He stood unmoved by her punishment; the crow's-feet in the corners of his eyes grew more compressed, but the bland expression on his face never changed.

"Stupid dogs!" she shouted with such contempt, even the hardest man in their ranks gave a shudder. "That bastard was in your grasp and you let him get away!"

Only the sounds of the weary horses snorting could be heard. Then one of the jaded animals went down to his knees and with a loud grunt died before he even spilled onto his side in the dust. His rider, caught off guard, stood, holding the reins and blinking in disbelief at the demise of his mount. Then, wide-eyed, he looked around to the others for some kind of an answer—no one dared flinch.

"He was fine—" he mumbled.

Her boot heels clicked on the hard-baked dirt as she raced across the porch, the quirt drawn back, and lashed at him. Under her continued vicious attack, he threw up his hands to protect his face and head from the three strips of shot-loaded leather she flailed him with.

"Stupid." Each word punctuated with a slash of her multi-tailed quirt, back and forth she whipped him. "Dumb! Ignorant! Donkey! Ass!

"Can't you see you killed that horse?" she demanded.

On his knees, holding his arms protectively over his head against any further attack, he mumbled, "I know. I know."

"I should whip all of you," she said and stomped back to the porch.

At the open French doors, she turned and looked at them. "Get fresh horses and go look again. I want his head brought to me in a sack."

"*Si,* señorita," Matamoris said and waved for the others to go to the corrals.

"Don't you dare leave that dead horse in my yard either."

"*Si,* señorita."

"That bastard Slocum is somewhere out there. Find him and bring me his head."

"*Si,* señorita."

She disappeared inside the great house. The sounds of her angry voice carried to them outside. Wildly, she issued orders to her domestics, followed by the screams of some poor maid who caught the edge of her quirt.

Matamoris led his spent gelding toward the corral. Some of their animals would have to be shot; they'd never recover. Like the dead horse who escaped her ire by his death, only in the next world would there be any peace for any of them.

He touched two fingers to his cheek and the sight of red blood on the tips was enough. The smart from the tails of the whip remained on his skin. He studied a pair of buzzards riding the hot air, circling, already anxious for a feast on the dead horse.

"Someone has gone for the mules to pull away the carcass," Gilberto said to him.

He nodded that he heard the man. Good, they would handle it. Still seething with rage, he glanced back at the sprawling house and the hump lying on the ground that once bore a man. He considered this one called Slocum, who only a few weeks before had saddled up and rode out under one of her tirades—but what terrible thing had he done to her to deserve this much hatred? Perhaps he would never know. Except the man was a ghost and gone like smoke—the one they sought must be a spirit.

1

Three vultures rode the hot air currents. Slocum noted them. Only scouts looking for their next meal. He rode the narrow trail that snaked into the bowels of the deep canyon. The echo of his mustang's iron shoes on the rocky surface rang out like a series of bells. Nothing he could do about that. Several times since he started down the mountain, his right knee had scraped the sheer wall of pastel brown and forced him to draw it tight to the horse's side. To reassure his mount, he patted the small bay's neck; it was a thousand feet straight down on the other side of their narrow shelf.

At last, he reached a wide enough place to stop where the trail made a U-turn around an outcropping and dismounted on his sea legs to let the animal catch his breath. For a long moment, he held the saddle horn until the strength recovered in his lower limbs. Then he took off the straw hat and wiped his sweaty face on his gritty shirtsleeve. He glanced up the trail into the blinding sun glinting off the sparkling canyon side—no pursuit in sight.

The past month he had been hounded by several bounty men and a posse of vaqueros. Perhaps they'd all lost his scent. He hoped so. With the first cool breeze of the day sweeping his sweaty face, he could gaze over the vast space beneath him and across the way see the jumbled, tall mountains in their blue cast. Perhaps here in the vastness of the Sierra Madras, he could finally shake all the pursuit off his trail.

Mexico was his last sanctuary. He always went there to seek asylum from the bounty hunters on his trail in the States. But even that security had expired. Perhaps in these vast mountains, he could find some place of solace and rest for a while. He felt like a long-tailed cat in a room full of rockers in every place he stopped—this gut-wrenching uneasiness had to end somewhere.

With the side of his thumb, he cleaned the grit from the corners of his mouth. The sour smell of his unwashed body wafted up his nostrils. Life was too short to be away from the better things: a bath, something to drink, to eat and the subtle body of a sensuous woman in his arms. With a disgusted head shake at the state of his affairs, he checked the girth, then satisfied, he spoke to the pony, "Whoa."

His left foot in the stirrup, he swung aboard, checking for one last look at his back trail. Nothing. No sounds of pursuit. He nudged the bay on.

Hours later at the base of the mountain, he found a small stream that seeped through the round rocks underneath some cottonwood trees. He dismounted and led the horse to a small pool. On his belly beside him, horse and rider shared the cool liquid. Then he washed his face and, feeling somewhat revived, rose to his feet. The hungry bay went to grazing the dried grass nearby through his bit and Slocum let him.

Over his head, a chorus of birds sang. Small darting brown ones flew about and multicolored ones sat in the branches to warble. He listened to the gathering afternoon wind rustle the cottonwood leaves—a good place to rest for a short while. Besides, his slap-sided pony needed the nourishment from the grass.

In the shade, he napped on his back for a short while. Awakening to the sounds of hoofbeats approaching from the west, he felt for the Colt in the quick-draw holster in his lap.

A pack train possibly. But why was it coming out this way? There were few easy ways to reach any settlements if you went out like he came in. He rose to his feet to try to see what was coming. Then, unable to make it out, he went to the bay and gathered his reins.

At last, he spotted the first burro under a pack come into sight. Good, no armed guard, he quickly decided. Then the other pack animals came on the first one's heels. Several. Soon the peaked sombrero of the driver came into view. His dark brown face represented a blend of *Indio* and Hispanic. A smile softened his look of surprise.

"Buenos tardes," the man said, removing his hat.

"Good afternoon to you too," Slocum said in Spanish to the man.

"You scared me. I seldom see anyone for days on this trail, señor."

Slocum nodded and considered the man. "Then perhaps you didn't see me either."

"My lips are sealed." The man nodded in understanding. His burros halted, they stood hipshot under their loads. Tail switching at flies, they remained in line on the trail.

"So are mine."

"Good water here," the man in his thirties said in approval.

"Water your animals," Slocum said and pulled the bay aside.

"Gracias. What may I do for you?"

"A pinch of tobacco to smoke would be kind," Slocum said.

"Ah, I have some," the man said and produced corn shucks from the pouch slung over his shoulder.

"This is very generous of you," Slocum said in approval, taking a shuck.

The man put some fine-shredded tobacco on Slocum's U-formed wrapper. He rolled it up, twisted the end and produced a match from his vest pocket. When the driver finished making his own, Slocum struck it, lighting the man's first then his own.

The rich flavor quickly filled his mouth and he inhaled

deep. The smoke in his lungs, he felt the relief of the nicotine as it began to flow through his bloodstream. He nodded in approval to the man.

"Is there somewhere ahead where I may buy some food?"

"Cebeza De Vaca," he said and motioned to the south.

Head of the cow. Sounded like a great stopover. But what could he expect in these isolated mountains—so long as they had food there.

"A village?" he asked.

"A small one," the man said, bobbing his head and meaning not much.

"Have a safe journey," Slocum said and drew in on his smoke, savoring every draw.

"To you too, amigo. I have some *pulcia* I can spare."

"You have been too generous."

The man shook his head, went to the last pack, and drew out a long leather sack. "Here."

"May I pay you?"

The man shook his head. "May your days be many, amigo."

Slocum held up the pouch filled with the cornmeal and brown sugar mixture in appreciation. "The same to you, my new friend."

He remounted the bay and headed down the canyon, still wondering what the heavily laden animals were bearing in the packsaddles. Gold, contraband, he would probably never know. At the fork in the road, he noticed the sign in the tree crotch. On a weathered small board written in faded letters and an arrow, all done in charcoal—Vaca.

Here the live oak and juniper choked the canyon floor. Rich-colored, red-bark mountain mahogany brush filled in. He occasionally booted the bay to keep him moving down the narrow pathway. Under the shadow of the mountain and a fresh breeze sweeping the gorge, he rode on, wondering what awaited him in Vaca. Perhaps the sanctuary he sought. Only time would tell.

He passed two old men with their burros loaded with piles of branches to sell as firewood. They doffed their old hats to him and called him *"Patrón,"* A ways farther, he reined up as two young girls armed with sticks herded their darting goats off the trail for his passage.

He thanked them and they blushed, embarrassed. Looking away when he rode on, he heard them giggling behind his back.

Soon he could see a few scattered huts on the hillside and more tall cottonwoods. From the sounds there obviously was a good-sized stream that flowed out of the mountains at this place. He closed his gritty eyes for a moment. Perhaps this would be where he could rest and recover. He hoped so. A place called the Head of a Cow.

2

He tied the bay at the hitch rail. An adobe building with faded green bat-wing doors stood before him; no doubt these wings of civilization had been packed into these mountains by burros or mules. A cantina, he smiled to himself. Even in the back recesses of the Madras, there were places a man could buy a drink. Perhaps not bottle and bond, but at least some cactus juice poison to cut the trail dust from his throat.

"Ah, patron," a swarthy man behind the bar shouted when he entered the dark, shadowy interior. "What can I do for you?"

"I need a drink."

"Mescal do?"

"Fine," he said, looking around at the crude benches and tables made no doubt by some local craftsmen. There was no one else in the place. He dug in his pocket to pay the bartender, who brought him his liquor in a pottery cup.

"No glasses," the man said and shrugged. "They broke all of them bringing them. The mule fell off the trail." He shook his head, looking downcast. "My poor glasses were all broken."

"Kill the mule?"

"*Si,* but you can always raise another mule. I can't afford to buy no more glasses."

The potent liquor cut off Slocum's breath for a second. He nodded in approval at the man who asked for ten cents. He set the cup down and paid him.

"Is there a hotel here? Boardinghouse? Someone who takes in guests?"

The man made a pained face as if deep in thought. Then he tilted his head and finally began to nod. "Ah, there's the widow woman, Magdellania Flores, who might do that."

"Where is she?" he asked, studying the contents of the cup.

"You cross the river and ride upstream a ways. She has some open land on the right. Lots of flowers around her casa. You can't miss her place."

Slocum nodded he heard him, then he downed the rest of his cup, feeling it warm his ears and the entire way down to his empty stomach. "*Gracias.* I shall go find this Magdellania."

"Magdellania Flores."

"*Gracias.*" Outside in the bright sunshine, he squinted until his eyes adjusted. When he mounted up and headed for the river, he rode past a small mule going round and round on the end of a pole powering a millstone. A small boy wearing only shorts enforced the mule's gait with a whip and sharp words. The two grind rocks ground corn for a handful of waiting women.

Clear water rushed over the ford that came up to the bay's knees. A wide stream by Mexican mountain standards, Slocum wondered how many silver trout lurked in the river. Up the other bank, he nodded to a young woman with a jar on her head, en route to fill it from the source.

A few curs ran out to bark at him and dark-eyed children peeked after him. Towering cottonwood trees overhead provided cool shade. The trail led upstream, past some small fields of corn and gardens, with Slocum on the lookout for the flowers. He rounded a bend and there were the reds, blues and yellows of many blossoms. Nestled under some gnarled tree trunks sat a small adobe. He turned the bay toward it.

A straight-backed woman came out. Her dark eyes studied him as she swept the black hair back from her face. She had a shapely body, and she bore a regal manner.

"Señora Flores?" he asked.

She nodded, waiting for him to speak about the reason for his presence.

"The cantina owner said that perhaps I could board here."

With a twist of her long black hair in both hands beside her olive face, she remained still in deep consideration of his request.

"I've been on the trail several weeks. My pony and I both need to rest for a while." The bay lowered his head and punctuated his words with a long snort.

"Your name?"

"Slocum."

"Señor Slocum, welcome to my casa." She bowed her head.

"Slocum will do just fine," he said and dismounted. "Where may I put the bay here?"

"Come," she said, stepping in and taking his reins. "There's a hammock for your siesta in back. I will turn your horse loose to graze behind the house."

"I can unsaddle him—"

She shook her head. "No, señ—Slocum, you are my guest."

"May I call you Magdellania?" he asked over his shoulder after she insisted on following him.

"Yes, of course. There." She pointed to the hammock under the squaw shade, an open-sided shed made with four poles and a flat roof with brush piled on top to cut out the sun's rays.

"I can unsaddle him," he protested.

"Take a siesta. After that I will have the water heated for your bath."

"Very good," he said and undid his holster. He hung the harness on a post peg, then settled into the hammock. Not a bad-looking woman, perhaps in her late twenties. Nice cleavage under the low-cut white blouse, and the colorful full skirt showed she possessed a narrow waist and a nice turn to her ankles in the sandals as she led the pony away. He stretched out in the hammock and his eyes soon closed shut.

"Señor?" The whisper of her voice in his ear brought him to full awareness. The red fire of a dying sundown filled the area around the shade. He considered his pistol on the post.

"Yes?"

"Two men just rode by," she said.

"Who are they?"

"Reyas's men."

"They bandits?"

She nodded. "They come and extract taxes from everyone."

"Pistoleros?" he asked, but when he tried to sit up, her firm hand on his shoulder kept him down.

"Yes, but they will ride on. Stay in the swing."

"Hey, I can—"

Her finger on his lips silenced him. She shook her head. "They killed my husband. This is not your fight. You're my guest."

"Where are they now?"

"Probably the cantina. Ramon will pay them and give them drinks. Then they will ride on."

"How do you know they won't do more than that?"

She made a face as if she wondered how to tell him. "Once—two of his men got drunk here and the next day, two of them." She drew the side of her hand like a knife over her throat. "His men don't sleep here anymore."

"Have they harmed you?"

"They shot my husband in the back."

"You know this?" he asked.

She nodded.

"Where does this head bandit live?"

"At the silver mine." She made a motion toward the high country to the east. "Stay here. They will ride on."

He looked at the pinch under her slender nose. The deep

brown color of her lips and the pillowy-looking lower one. A small light scar showed on the cheekbone under her left eye. Her long, dark lashes and the deep brown of each iris fascinated him. The scarlet-orange flames of sundown danced on her smooth complexion; her handsome looks made his empty stomach roil.

"I promise I'll behave."

"Good," she said with a small smile for him and stood. "When they leave, you may bathe."

"I might smell better after that."

She nodded in agreement at his words. But he could tell that her center of attention and concern was focused toward the village. Despite her big talk, he figured she still worried what those two bandits might be doing over there. Was there no place on earth to escape scoundrels? Probably not—not even in the confines of the Sierra Madras.

They finally rode past on trotting ponies headed up the mountain for the mine she spoke of earlier. Slocum could hear their confident-sounding talk when they passed her place. Their extortion must have paid them well from the sounds of their words. He would see about that too.

When the two were gone, she had guided him to the tub filled with hot water and left him to his own devices. The hot bathwater in the wooden tub soaked into his pores. He used the cloth and soap she provided him. By himself in the darkness under the stars, he scrubbed off the layers of grit and grime.

He looked up at her return.

"Here's some clean pants to wear and a shirt on the bench. Tomorrow I will wash your clothes." With that said, she turned on her heel and went away.

The heated water made him drowsy despite the nap—it had been weeks since he dared do more than shut his eyes for a short while at any time. He wondered about those that hounded him. Were they still back there? The notion made him angry.

"Your food is ready," she announced discreetly from the darkness at edge of the shade.

"Be there," he said and rose, seeing the silhouette of her going back to the house. Drying himself, he wondered about her. Certainly, she was no ordinary widow in the hinterlands. He sat upon the bench and dried his feet. The soft pants had a drawstring and fit him. The pullover shirt was big enough too. They smelled fresh and felt good against his clean skin.

He put on the sandals set out with the clothing. With arms full of his boots, gun and sour-smelling clothing, he went to the soft glow of candles under the other squaw shade, of a type that some called a ramada.

He set the load down, then took the chair she indicated. The rich smell of her cooking soon filled his nose. On the handmade glazed plate before him, she dished out black beans, some fresh greens and pulled meat. Then she offered him some fresh corn tortillas. He took one, looking hard into the liquid centers of her eyes.

"For a stranger riding through, you treat me too good," he said.

"Ah, it is seldom I have such a guest at my casa."

"Word gets out about this, you'll be busy."

"What brings you to Vaca?" She poured him wine in a pottery cup.

He used the tortilla to point at the plate full of food. "This."

They both laughed.

While he ate the tasty food, he felt his desire for her growing. Looking across in the flickering light at her, he wondered how many men rode for this bandit she called Reyas. They killed her husband for what—objecting to their "taxes." Time would tell. About her and Reyas. Meanwhile he wanted to savor every bite of her tasty fare, the symphony of the night wind in the rustling cottonwood leaves, insects and this moment of peace.

3

He awoke in the predawn to the loud proclamation of a red-and-black rooster on the roof of the shade. His first thought was to blast the vocal, feathered male to kingdom come with his pistol, then a smile replaced his frown and he threw his legs over the edge. It had been years since a cockerel had awoke him. He looked around in the half-light; she was squatted near her fire hole busy bringing it to life with small twigs.

"Coffee in a little while," she said.

"Good." When she turned away, he rose and put on the cotton pants, then the shirt and the sandals. He crossed the floor to where she worked.

"Tell me about this Reyas," he said, kneeling down beside her.

"He rules these mountains. I am surprised that you even rode in here. His men usually guard all the trails."

"Maybe they let me in," he said, looking around in the half-light to certain they were alone.

"They will know you are here soon enough, I suspect." She wrinkled her nose. "He pays spies to tell him everything."

"Are there no *federales*?"

"They never come to this village. Maybe Reyas buys them off." She hung the kettle on a hook over the fire to heat. "You should ride on. What happens in Vaca is not your concern."

"What if I make it mine?"

"Sure, so I can bury your carcass too." She shook her head in disapproval. "I am tired of funerals."

"I don't intend to die."

"Neither did my husband."

"Are there no people left to resist?"

"I don't think so," she said, putting a blackened square of sheet iron over the fire.

Soon her cut-up squash, onions, sweet and hot peppers sizzled on the stovetop. Then she made corn tortillas, only thicker ones than the night before, and when they began to brown, she turned them with her fingertips. From a basket, she took out eggs, scrambled them with the rest and stirred the yellow concoction on the grill top. Then, opening the center of the first cake, she crammed in some of the mixture and handed him a filled one.

Shocked at the heat of the patty, he tossed the cake from hand to hand until he could stand the touch of it. She laughed at him, busy making more of the stuffed ones without a hot holder.

"It will cool soon enough," she said.

He ate his breakfast of stuffed cakes and drank her rich coffee. Stuffed so full, at last, he held up his hands when she offered him more. "Enough."

"You can take some with you when you ride out of here."

"Who said I was going?"

She looked at him sharply in disapproval. "I will not cry at your funeral." Then, as if affronted, she rose to her feet and fled into the jackal.

He wondered how he had so easily alienated her. Her husband's death, no doubt, was still fresh on her mind. Oh, well, whoever this Reyas was, he might need to meet him. Stretching his hands over his head, he walked over to the shade post and strapped on his holster. It was one thing for bandits to hold up harmless country people for protection fees and another for them to face a man with a gun.

She came out with his clothes in her arms. "I am going to wash them, so you will not look like a peon at your funeral."

"Fine, I'll go along and watch." He put on his straw hat and followed her. She walked quickly. Being unused to the sandals, he was forced to hurry in them to keep up with her.

At the stream, she chose a place in the shallows and knelt in the water. He sat upon a rounded boulder of white granite and looked around. Several other women were doing their washing and cut curious glances at her and him. Some whispered and others laughed aloud as if they had learned a secret. Then sharply they swallowed their amusement, looking away embarrassed as they worked, kneading their clothing in the stream. Clean items were tossed aside and the next items dunked. Then the wet ones were wrung out and spread to dry in the sun on the smooth rocks.

"Magdellania?" a young woman of perhaps eighteen called to her. She nodded to Slocum in passing by, holding up her skirt to expose her shapely brown legs. She waded into the shallow water to get Magdellania's attention.

"They left word yesterday at the cantina. Some of Reyas's men are coming to celebrate this Saturday and we must entertain them."

Magdellania sat back on her heels and made a pained face at the woman. "They said what? They can roast in hell before I would do that with them."

"They will expect you to be there," the girl said, sounding concerned.

"I am not their *puta*."

"Things are different—now," the girl said.

"You mean since my husband was killed by those bastards."

"Yes . . ."

"When I open my whorehouse, they can pay for it," Magdellania said and went back to vigorously surging his pants in the water.

"Oh, please don't make trouble. They will hurt all of us."

Then Magdellania twisted and glared at Slocum. "See why you must leave?"

"I've been listening. I savvy Spanish."

"You have an army?" she asked, looking insistent at him.

He raised his eyebrows. She had a point. One man, one pistol wasn't much, but damned if he could swallow the idea of this Reyas's kingdom business.

"I'm thinking."

"So did he," she said sharply and went to beating his pants on the rocks. Water splashed all over her, making her dollar-size nipples point through the soaked material of her blouse.

"Oh, Magdellania," the woman begged, wringing her hands. "Please don't make them angry."

She shook her head to dismiss the pleading girl, who in her upset state had let go of her dress tail to dip into the water. "Do what you must, Maria."

Ashen-faced, Maria chewed on her lower lip as she straightened and, holding up her wet dress hem, wobbled over the round rocks to the shore. Then crying, she hurried away.

He listened to the rush of the stream. The washwomen down the streamside were deathly silent; some had begun to gather their clothes, some of it even unwashed, and leave. When Magdellania finished, she wrung out his pants with vengeance. Then in anger she tossed them at him.

"See why I want you to leave?"

He caught them with both hands and met her glare. Holding them up, he shook out the wrinkles. "I figure I need to be here for that party."

"Oh—you are a dumb fool!" She jerked his denim pants from him and swept up his shirt and socks. With a quick look up at the azure sky for heavenly intervention, he rose and hurriedly followed her back to her place, a few lengths behind her stilted half run.

She slung his clothing over an arbor. He stood waiting behind her. So close that when she straightened, he was in her face.

"How many will come?"

"A dozen."

"Poison them," he said.

She blinked, narrowed her eyes and then slowly smiled. "Why didn't I think of that?"

"Cause you aren't mean enough yet. You said they don't sleep here for fear of getting their throats cut. Your people simply have not made believers out of them yet."

"Word gets out of the plan, someone will warn them."

"No one needs to know but you."

She pressed her fingertips to her temples. "How can we do it?"

"Now you're talking," he said and swept her in his arms.

She looked taken aback at his move. Realizing he had pressed for a liberty she was not ready to accept, he set her down on her feet again. He released her and shrugged. "How to poison them is next."

"A weed or herb that would give them dysentery?" She stepped back with an obvious quake of her shoulders.

"Good for starters. If you don't have hemlock."

She frowned in disapproval. "That would kill them."

"Try yours first, mine second." He decided he needed to give her some more room and time. Pacing back and forth, he began to list the things that worked. "Slippery elm bark boiled down."

"None of that grows in these mountains." She looked hard across the flowers and garden holding her arms folded over her chest and squeezing her chin on her fingers. "Dogbane, locoweed and some blue lupine would do that."

"Do we need to go find them?" he asked.

"Yes."

"I'll go saddle the horse. He can carry double."

"Fine. I will get some things and sacks, so we can carry it back."

"Sure," he said and set out for the bay.

The pony caught and saddled, she came on the run from the jackal to join him. Excitement glistened in her eyes. She tied the sacks on the horn while he finished cinching up. In the saddle, at last, he hoisted her up behind him and she pointed the way.

They rode downstream, drawing the looks of a few washerwomen and screaming naked children splashing in the water. She indicated for him to keep going and not turn toward the cantina and store across the ford. For several miles, they followed the river, then she directed him up a side canyon.

In a meadow of brown grass, she slipped from the horse and hurried to search the edge, looking to both sides as she went. To him this appeared to be a poor place to look for any herbs, but when she waved, he booted the bay over.

"Here is the locoweed," she said and dropped to her knees to gather the vetch-like vines. No plant expert, he knew most of the edibles to survive. This plant when consumed would make a horse crazy; lots of times an animal that had grazed it would be fine until they got hot. Then they'd become unmanageable, even rearing and falling over backward on their rider. One horse he owned that supposedly had eaten the locoweed had fits for no reason, like after a long ride, he would simply explode.

He drew out the large knife from the sheath behind his back and began to help her harvest the plants dotted with small white flowers. It was a tough, woody vine that surprised him with a specific sharp odor when cut. She stuffed it in the first sack while he sheared it off close to the ground by the handfuls.

Soon she touched his arm. "Enough."

The sack tied on, they remounted the bay and Slocum turned him back toward the stream. When they reached the rushing water, she told him to cross the swift river. In places the water was over the bay's knees during their ford, but they soon scrambled up the loose bank and were on a long, grassy flat. Pointing past him, he nudged the pony in the direction where she indicated.

The dogbane grew in small colonies. It rose a couple of feet tall; he recalled seeing it before. Some people even made rope from the fibers of the plant. She slid off the horse to the ground and asked for his knife when he joined her.

"This has sap that may irritate you. I'll cut it and you stuff it in the bag," she said and squatted down to slash off the plants.

"What about you," he asked.

She shook her head. "No problem, I have harvested it before."

The herb finally gathered, he had two sacks sharing the horn when they remounted and rode down the meadow. Following a narrow trail, they went through some live oak thickets and scared a small herd of javelinas, the piglike creatures of the southwest. The peccaries ran away into the brush with a few sharp barks.

Slocum and her ducked their heads for a low branch; they soon rode into a meadow of purple lupine. The flowers gleamed in the midday sunshine. He reined up and studied the tall mountain's soaring peaks before dismounting to help her.

"These bad too?"

"Yes," she said as he squatted on his boot heels and harvested the foot-tall plants.

"How will you keep the other women out of this stuff?"

"Good question. If I warn them, someone might tell the men. I'll have to work on that."

"That enough?" he asked as she finished stuffing the sack.

"Plenty, we can go back. Thank you," she said and then looked at the ground. "I will be deeply indebted to you before long."

Good," he said, on his second attempt to remount. "I'd like that."

In the saddle, he dropped his arm down and pulled her up, swinging her behind him. The pony was covered in riders and bulging sacks when they started back. He listened to the *whit-woo* of the small blue mountain quail—pretty call. Anxious to get back to her place, he booted the bay for the road.

Under the high midday sun, he felt a little drowsy and wondered about Evon—Evon Peralta—as he rode. The most spoiled woman in Mexico, she went around ordering everyone and slashing man and beast with her quirt. However, she only struck him once with it and he took the damn whip away from her. He was so angry with her actions, he jerked off her skirt and beat her bare butt with the handle.

And such a fiery woman in bed too. In abandoned fury, her fingernails clawed his back like a wildcat. Those dark, sleepy eyes that could turn to hate so fast were melted to dazzled each time after they had wild, gratifying sex in her great feather bed. Dreamily she sprawled on her back, muttering to him, her long, firm breasts like hard rocks shaking with her every move.

Morning sunlight speared in the room. Alone in the bed, the spot beside him was still warm to his touch where she had lain. He listened to her swearing at a servant down the hallway. The scream of the girl told him Evon had struck her with the quirt. Filled with anger, he bolted out of the great bed and hit the floor in his bare feet. Hastily pulling on his britches, he stuck his head out the doorway, searching for her as he buttoned them.

In the living room, Evon stood over the girl sprawled on the floor at her feet, crying with her arms overhead to defend herself from the quirt tails. He wrenched the whip from Evon's hand and spun her around. Anger and shock contorted the lovely face into one of ugly hatred.

"That's enough!" he said.

"Who are you to tell me my business?" she demanded.

"No one." He started back for his things. Enough of this whip-crazy woman—she would never learn. He would ride on.

"Where are you going?" she screeched like a fishwife after him.

"Away from you." He glanced back at her.

"You can't leave me." Lines of disbelief furrowed her smooth forehead.

"Try and stop me. Here's your whip." He tossed it at her feet.

"I'll have you killed!"

"You won't be the first to try that." Back in the room, he

dressed and strapped on his holster. He put on his hat and started past her.

Ahold of his arm, she planted her bare feet on the tile floor to keep him from leaving her.

"I'm leaving," he said, prying her fingers loose.

"No! No!" she screamed.

"Quiet, you'll wake the dead." He frowned at her.

"This is my hacienda! This is my house! I can scream if I want to." Then in her fury, she slapped him hard across the face. In an instant, she shrunk back. "I'm sorry—I-I didn't mean—"

"Good day, Evon," he said in a voice so cold, he felt the edge of it. The smart of her blow slowly evaporated from the side of his face.

He went down the hall and out of the house. There was no dealing with such a spoiled, angry woman. Ignoring her frantic shouts from the house, he crossed the dusty, bare yard for the corral and his horse.

"Gawdamn, you donkey-dicked bastard! You can't leave me!" she screamed at the top of her lungs from the French doors. "I say when you can leave! No one ever leaves Evon Peralta and lives. You gringo *bastardo!* I'll see you in hell for this!"

"Maybe there," he said in a soft voice to the dun horse, cinching up the girth. "Yes, maybe in hell, Evon. That will be our next reunion."

Her caterwauling and cursing carried across the yucca-clad hills. She clung to a porch pole and screamed her threats of vengeance at him. He touched his hat and rode away, ignoring it. There had been several passionate women in his life, but for such a fiery one she sure made lots of trouble.

"Too late," Magdellania said under her breath, bringing him back from his daydreams as she reached past him for the reins to stop the horse. "Reyas's men up there have already seen us."

He glanced ahead and spotted the two riders. Both of them had reined up their horses and blocked the trail. Cursing his absentmindedness, if he hadn't been daydreaming about that wicked Evon, he'd noticed them sooner. Damn.

4

Estevan Reyas sat in the great wheel-back chair behind the desk and studied the peon before him. The prisoner looked downcast standing between the two guards. Reyas was a large-framed man for a Hispanic. He smoothed his thick mustache with the end of his index finger and considered how he must handle this situation.

"They say you have been high grading ore at the mine, Juan?" he accused the man.

The twenty-year-old's eyes grew round as saucers. "No, *Patrón*. I would never steal from you."

"They found some at your casa."

Juan shook his head, close to tears. "I never steal."

"What is this pouch?" he demanded and poured the sparkling yellow flakes into his palm.

Drawing his head back and shaking his head in fear, Juan said, "That's not mine. I don't know who put it in my house."

"Stealing from the mine is punishable by death."

"I never stole from you, *Patrón*." The man's head quaked in denial. Big tears cascaded down his dark cheeks.

"Perhaps you wish to think more about this," Reyas said.

"Take him to his cell. Perhaps that will improve his memory."

The two guards dragged the sobbing peon out of the room. When they were gone, Reyas stood up.

"I will return," he said to his clerk, Alphanso, and went outside. A stable boy hurried over with the high-headed, black Andalusian stallion saddled and ready for the chief.

"Do you wish bodyguards," his out-of-breath clerk asked from the porch.

"Not today," he said, mounting swiftly and reining up the dancing stud with the severe curb bit. He spun him around and flew out of the open yard. Hooves clattering, he scattered children, chickens and dogs in the small village street until he reined him up before the small casa of the prisoner, Juan, and Reyas dismounted. The head-tossing stallion pranced around him, screaming his challenge to any who could hear. The stud's defiance drew a small grin to Reyas's hard-set lips. He tied his reins to a cart wheel and strode to the doorway.

His hand on the rough-hewed facing, he called for her. "Annette?"

"*Patrón,* what do you want?" she asked, rushing to the doorway to meet him. Her eyes were red-rimmed from crying. The slip of a girl dressed in a plain skirt and blouse stood with her head bowed.

He stepped inside and crooked a finger at her. "Come here." Her eyes widened and she obeyed, taking hesitant steps toward him.

"Juan's life depends on you and how good you act," he said and with his hands on her shoulders, he forced her to kneel.

Then he undid his pants and let them fall. She gave a small cry. One hand holding the back of her head, he forced her to open her mouth and accept him. For a long while, he savored her clumsy treatment, then he took her by the nape of the neck and raised her up. Scooting his feet along the gritty floor with his pants trapping his ankles, he took her to the blankets on the floor. There he forced her to undress and lie down.

Embarrassed, pale with fear, she cowered on the pallet. He roughly spread her legs apart and moved between them. A small whimper escaped her lips when he drove his huge dick inside her. Then he pleasured himself on top of her. Finished at last, he rose up, wiped his slick, dying manhood off on her blouse, which he then tossed aside.

"Get your things. Come to my casa. I need a plaything like you." When she turned her face away from him, he caught her chin and drew her close. "He only lives as long as you do what I say. You savvy?"

She nodded woodenly, and he released her. With the flat of his hand, he slapped her hard on her bare behind. "You ain't bad for a beginner. But I'll teach you how to really pleasure a man."

Then he drew up his pants and looked around with scowl. "Don't be long getting up there to my casa either."

She nodded, looking like a small fox caught in a trap, wild and ready to flee. Only he held the ace card. He had her new husband, Juan, in a cell.

Reyas rode back to the office in a carefree mood. His empire worked smoothly as long as he kept the upper hand. The workers in the mine behaved or they knew what they faced— his wrath—and none of them wanted to even hear it. He chuckled aloud, amused by all of his power over these stupid people as he trotted his stallion through the small village. Women averted their eyes from him when he rode past. They knew about his own reputation as a stud.

He laughed some more over his own macho image.

High on the mountain over him, the mine activity looked busy enough. Workers were bringing out crude carts of rich ore to load into panniers and dumping others filled with blasted rock onto the growing pile that sloped down the mountainside toward his office and compound. The high-grade ore would be sent north to the States for refining. No tariff was charged on straight ore so he could send it up there to be refined without any duty. He sent such material out by burro trains over back trails, so they hardly looked worth the trouble to rob. The method saved him the cost of armed guards and hired guns that were expensive. So far the system had worked well.

When he dismounted at his office, he handed the reins to the stable boy. The great black stallion danced around, curling his lip out as if in quest of some red-hot mare in heat. Then the stud's huge penis appeared underneath his belly and Reyas nodded in approval as the boy stopped, holding the reins close. The big horse began to hunch and soon a fizzle of white foam spouted from the enlarged head that fanned out like a huge sunflower.

"Ah, like mine," Reyas said to himself and bounded up the stairs for his office. Time for his siesta, and he began to think of his plans for his new love thing—Annette. Aw, such a tender thing.

"Colonel Reyas," Alphanso, his clerk of perhaps eighteen, said, awakening him from his siesta. "They have a gringo outside."

"They?" he asked, pained, swinging his legs over the side of the hammock.

"Manuel and Torga."

"Hmm," he grunted out his nose. Who was this gringo?

"They say he was with the widow Flores in Vaca."

"A good choice of woman." He ran his fingers through his thick black hair and smoothed it down on the sides. How did this gringo ride in without notice? Two of his men were in Vaca the day before collecting his fees. Why had they not learned about this intruder?

He combed his hair back again and went to the front doorway. From where he stopped, he could see the tall man standing at the hitch rack acting disinterested. When the gringo finally looked up, his dark eyes tried to bore a hole in him.

"What is your business here?" Reyas demanded.

"My own."

"What is his name?" he asked Torga.

"Slo-cum, they say."

"Well, Slo-cum, you rode into my land uninvited. You take up with a lovely widow and you say you are here on your own business."

"Gawdamn, I looked on the map. Said this was Mexico. You the *presidente*? This Mexico City?"

"I am the owner of this land."

"Ah, that's good. But you don't run the courts and the laws."

"In these mountains, I am the law." He felt the anger rise so fast in his chest he felt a pain knife at him from under his ribs.

"Guess you've got official papers and all that?"

"I don't need no stinking papers. This is my land, my mine and these mountains are mine." He stood upright and threw out his aching chest. "You're going to learn about my land. Throw him in a cell."

"Guess old Captain Debrewski and his troops will be here in three or four days or so. Reckon you can tell him then that his chief scout is in your jail."

"Debrewski? Why is he coming?" Reyas hated the sound of this man's name. The Ruralist captain was not someone he wished to meet face-to-face either.

" 'Cause the governor of Sonora heard about your little deal up here."

"You're bluffing."

"Try me. Cap'n ain't going to take lightly your boys roughing me up either. I know him well."

Torga looked at his boss. "What should we do with him?"

"Give him his gun and horse. But, Slo-cum, if you're lying to me, I'm going to personally cut your balls out."

"Hey, that ain't half what my boss'll do to you for all this business of extortion you've been doing and slave labor up there at the mine."

Another knife under his ribs stabbed Reyas. He drove his thumb hard against his breastbone to stop it and glared at the gringo. "You better ride out before I change my mind."

"Don't worry about me. It's your own ass you better be

for saving." Slocum stepped in the stirrup and swung up on the bay. Torga handed him the Colt back.

He reined up the bay and looked them over. "Nice meeting you three. Hope you like four walls and bars, 'cause they've got some waiting for you and all your men."

Reyas ground his molars together. His fists clenched so tight that his fingers ached. The pain in his right arm made him nauseated as he watched the man short lope down the road, doffing his hat to a woman. That clown better be Debrewski's man or he'd shred him like tobacco.

"Patrón? Patrón?" Torga called, breaking into his consciousness. "Should we follow him?"

"No, come in here." He turned on his heel and went back in the office. The two henchmen walked in behind him with their hats in front of them, floured in trail dust.

"First—" He stopped and motioned for Torga to close the office door. "I want that Juan in the jail killed. His body hid or buried so no one finds him." He let a great exhale out his nose, still enraged by the nerve of that Slo-cum. "That woman of his, Annette, is coming here. Take and kill her too and hide her body. You truly understand what hiding their bodies means?" His eyelids narrowed as he demanded their attention to his orders.

"Si, Patrón."

"How many more are there in this camp who would talk to Debrewski if he comes?" he asked, pacing back and forth on the office floor.

"You think he is coming?"

"Yes, I think Debrewski might come here. That gringo *bastardo* maybe lying too, but we can't take any chances."

"Maybe that Raverez woman."

"Yes. Strangle her tonight and bury her in the graveyard tomorrow. Who else?"

"What about the Flores widow? Her husband must be the one who sent word about us to the governor of Sonora."

Reyas considered the notion. "He could have. We waited too long. How would we kill her with that Slo-cum so close?"

"Maybe Durango could think of a way." Manuel smiled at his own words.

Scratching through the hair on the back of his neck, Reyas considered what he must do next. His life had been so perfect when he went to take his siesta, now everything had gone to hell in less than an hour and blasted away all his dreams of holding this empire forever.

His money was safely deposited in the Silver City bank up in the U.S. Not all of it, but plenty enough for him to live in the States for the rest of his life like a great *patrón*. But there were millions more he could still make out of this mine—the vein of good ore was still easy to reach. No flooding yet like those Tombstone mines were plagued with. One tough *pistolero* rides in and he must run like a rabbit. Not fair, not fair at all.

"Tell Durango to get up here," he said, recalling Manuel's suggestion. That ugly hired gun would rather kill someone than eat.

"I will. Should we post more guards?" Torga asked.

"Yes, we do need to cover our ass. We must know when those Ruralists come in here. Torga, you, Manuel, Durango and the others, I will pay fat bonuses to all of you, if you stay loyal. I promise that we will all get out of here before Debrewski can arrive to ask the first question."

"Si, Patrón." Both men grinned and left.

In a short while, the lanky form of Durango came sauntering into his office. Looking half asleep, he smiled and showed his two missing teeth.

"You need me, boss?"

Obviously this degenerate was the nighttime product of some red-haired gringo and a mostly *Indio* border whore. Durango's hair looked a dusty orange, uncombed and mussed up on his head. Freckles covered most of his face, but the blotches of white in between were like scars. No whiskers, only a few long reddish blond hairs under his nose, and beneath it were the fat lips of a mule. The green-eyed *pistolero* slouched while standing before him. He did the same when he walked, stood around, or sat in the saddle—they even said he slouched when he was screwing a woman.

"I want that Flores woman out of the way for good," Reyas said.

Durango's head bobbed in agreement; he showed the two empty spaces in his front teeth and laughed aloud. A silly laugh, kind of shrill and like a screech owl on the end escaped his ugly mouth.

"She's with that scout for Debrewski named Slocum. Be careful. I'll need you."

"I got to kill that Raverez woman first. I told Torga"—he tossed his head toward the door—"I'd do it for him."

"Makes no difference, I want both of them bitches gone before Debrewski gets here."

"Yeah, they will be. Sure will be. I promise you. I ever not get it done for you?"

"No, you're one of my most trusted men. I'll pay you a big bonus when this is over."

Durango threw his arms in the air and made a small cloud of dust. "Hell, I'd kill them two for nothing." Then the funny laugh escaped his mouth; it drew goose bumps on the skin over Reyas's shoulders.

"Good, you handle it. But don't mess with that scout unless you have to. Do you savvy?" Why was he being so protective of the gringo? It was common information everyone knew well, but lingered hard in his mind. If anyone ever killed a Ruralist or was even vaguely involved in such a murder they would be killed instantly on the spot by the troops upon their capture.

"Hell. I hear yuh good. Them two are good as dead." Durango snapped his fingers to emphasize his point, then he jerked on his sombrero and sauntered out of the office.

Reyas sniffed the air. A strong fecal odor still hung in the office; damn, did the red-headed bastard even wipe his ass? Whew, it smelled bad in his office even without him being in there.

Before Reyas fled this place, he needed two more pack trains loaded with ore headed north—it would be that much more money in the bank up there. Might be his last ones.

Once they were on their way, there wasn't much way to stop the trains.

What a fucking shame. Another ten years and he could have had enough money to buy railroads or a ship line. Maybe he could come back—no, once he left here, if he valued his life, he needed to stay over the border, living the life of some big horse rancher. Already he had the fine stallions in his stables.

It was a shame he didn't have a classy woman to run his house. That Flores bitch would work for looks. Straight-backed, Castilian-looking, she'd do good for impressive meetings and functions. On the side, he could screw all the maids like that Annette he'd worked on that afternoon. Being out of these prison-like mountains wouldn't be so bad, with nothing to do but watch his high-priced foals hit the ground and screw all the gringo women he wanted.

What was that scout's name—Slocum. They would cross paths again. He would put out some feelers. For a few hundred pesos, he could hire his ass dropped in a well. He'd do just that when this was over and he was safe in Silver City, living the good life. He smiled to himself. Then he would put out a contract for Slocum's death.

5

"You did what?" Magdellania asked, aghast.

"I told him that Ruralists were on their way up here and I was one of Captain Debrewski's scouts."

She frowned in disbelief. "And he turned you loose?"

He jerked the saddle off the bay. "He wanted no part of Debrewski. Now all we need to do is get word to the captain to come up here."

"But how? Reyas's men guard the passes in and out of here."

"First, is there a dependable young man in the village who would ride with a message to the captain?"

"I suppose."

"Good, then we need your tea to give to those guards."

"Tea?"

"The poison."

"I almost forgot about that. But I don't know how much to give them."

He held the saddle in both hands, ready to toss it on the fence when they worked the details out. "Give them plenty. We need some young girls to take it to them. For them to act willing to seduce them until the poison sets in, anyway."

She scowled in disbelief at him. "What if it don't work?"

"Don't send virgins."

She looked at the sky for help and waved her head from side to side as if she thought him out of his mind. "You have some crazy ideas."

"It's better than what they had planned for the women Saturday night."

"Yes, but this will never work." She shook her head in disappointment.

Tired of holding the saddle in his hands, he set it on the horn at his feet "Listen, it is the only thing that might work. Go find a boy with a good horse. We need to fix him up with some food, blankets and a pistol—in case."

"In case of what?"

"He runs into bandits."

"I'll go to the village and find that. Girls too?"

"Yes, and we need to be certain that Reyas's spies don't find out."

She dropped her shoulders. "Oh, yes, how will I do that?"

"If we want to live through this whole thing, then we better find out who is telling them things."

"We could post a guard on the road to the mine and stop anyone who tries to go up there?"

"That's thinking, girl. Now go get the help."

Magdellania returned in an hour. He raised up from the hammock and threw his legs over at her approach.

"How did it go?" he asked, combing his hair through his fingers and trying to shake the sleepiness from his head.

"Three young women will take the brew to the guards at the south entrance. We are going to mix it in some cafe."

"Good idea."

"The boy is Hernando. He can ride like an Apache. He use to be a captive of theirs and will be very good for this ride."

"You've done well. When do we make the try to get past them?"

"Tonight, we all meet at the edge of the village at dark.

The boy, Hernando, can ride out the south way."

"Can he find his way to look for Debrewski?"

She nodded sharply. "Oh, yes, he knows where to ride to."

"What about a horse?"

"We thought yours. To borrow one or steal one would sure get the word right away to Reyas."

"Good idea."

"I'm sorry, I know that will leave you afoot—but—"

"The bay can carry him." If he needed another one to ride out of there on, he'd steal it from Reyas.

Darkness settled in the deep canyon. They forded the river on his bay and rode downstream. At a small jackal, they met inside without light. Slocum could scent the other women's musk in the shadowy room as they whispered questions to him and Magdellania.

"Hernando," he said to the short youth. "You must deliver this letter to Captain Debrewski himself. Not to any aids or guards."

"*Si,* señor."

"You know where you may find him?"

"I will look at Fronteras first."

"Good, maybe someone will know of his whereabouts there if he is in the field."

"*Si.*"

"Here is some money. Be careful." He handed the youth his own pocket change. Enough to buy some food on his way, though Magdellania had filled the saddlebags with provisions for the youth. "Tell the captain all our lives depend on him coming here at once."

"I will, señor."

"We will make the way out of here safe for you," a young woman promised the youth.

"Good," he said.

"We will head for the pass," Magdellania said. "I will give you three flashes when to come."

"I'll stay close enough to see what happens," Slocum said.

"You should wait back with the boy."

"I'm part of this team," he said.

"Suit yourself."

"Hernando will wait back a ways with the bay."

"As you say," the boy said.

The women set out, ahead of the two males, the girls whispering and with a few laughs that sounded more nervous than as if they were having fun.

Slocum left the messenger and horse at the base of the mountain. Magdellania instructed her helpers to begin singing and laughing going up the steep trail as they drew closer to the guard's position.

"Are there any lovers up there?" one girl asked aloud.

No answer. Either they weren't close enough or the guards weren't on duty. Overhead a spray of stars filled the clear night's sky. If only this plan would work—a lot counted on it.

Slocum trailed on their heels, hand ready on the Colt's butt. The poison would be better. A shoot-out would only warn Reyas. He would suspect little this way. The boy's departure for help needed to be undetected until it was too late. One thing that made Slocum feel better was the fact Reyas's toughest *pistoleros* would not be on the gates.

"Who is there?" a voice at last challenged them.

"Theresa and my friends," one of the girls answered. "Can we come up there?"

"Ah, *si*," the man shouted, sounding excited at the prospect of their visit.

Magdellania stopped Slocum with her arm. "Let them go first. We can sneak up later and watch."

He agreed, seeing the glow of the guards' campfire. The two of them sat down and the three women went on.

"My, this hill is steep," one of the women said.

"Ah, there will be great lovers up there," another said.

"Yes, yes," shouted a man's voice. "*Mucho grande* lovers are up here."

The girls laughed at his words. Their sandals crunched the gravel on the trail.

"We brought a big surprise," Theresa shouted.

"What?"

"Tiswain."

"Ah, wonderful!" a man cried out. *"Tiswain* and lovely señoritas. Did Reyas send you for us?"

"You can guess who sent us," Theresa said and the men laughed.

Soon the sounds of a guitar broke the night and many cheers went up. Obviously someone was hat dancing to the quick strumming. The applause and the click of castanets soon came to where Slocum and Magdellania sat in the darkness.

"Now they are distracted. Let's get closer," she whispered and they began the steady climb up the steep path, staying close to the wall.

Soon they could make out in the fire's light the three men drinking the *tiswain* and shouting how good it tasted. One of the girls had her arms around a man's waist, cheering him on as they weaved around the fire. Another was holding a mug to the lips of the guitar player. The third guard held his cup in one hand and with his other hand he openly felt the breast of the girl beside him.

"Drink," she said and pushed the container to his mouth. "It will make you hard."

He obeyed, taking a great swallow and then following with an "ah."

The one weaving around soon went to his knees. He clung to her and then buried his face in her skirt. When he spilled down, she went after him on the ground as if anxious to have him. Her hands ripped open his pants and soon she pulled on his root, to cover his unconscious condition from the others.

Magdellania nodded in approval as she and Slocum bellied down side by side under a juniper. "The guitarist is getting dizzy."

Slocum nodded in approval. "It's working."

The one feeling the girl's breast suddenly buckled in his knees and he fainted away too. Slocum and Magdellania stood to share a nod of approval.

"I'll get the boy," he said.

"We must wipe out any tracks," she reminded him. "They must not know that he left."

Slocum agreed.

Durango eased himself inside the back door into the inky house's interior. The great knife in his right hand, small glints of the starlight reflected from the polished blade. Sophie Raverez was a woman of thirty, short with full hips. He knew her body well from the times past when he had screwed her, but ever since her husband, Sanchez, died in the "mine accident," only the *patrón* had used her ripe body. This would be fun. A smile on his full lips, he crossed the room listening to her soft breathing. She lay upon a feather bed, no doubt a gift from Reyas—few workers could afford such a luxury.

He toed off his boots, making little noise. Then he set down the knife, and drawing the holster belt up, he took the buckle apart and gently let it fall to the ground. With his galluses off his shoulders, he unbuttoned his pants, feeling the stirring already in his privates for her. The britches on the floor, he began to jack off his half-erect dick.

Satisfied it would work, he moved to the bed. Cat-like, he pounced on her. She awoke with his calloused hand clamped over her mouth. Her dark eyes dancing as he smothered off any scream.

"Be quiet or else," he said from on top of her, forcing her legs part with his knees.

"Reyas will kill you," she hissed under his palm, trying to squirm from under him.

Durango laughed aloud. "You think I fear him. Lie still, you bitch."

"No."

Anger blinded him with rage at her insolence. Both of his hands clutched tight her throat; he shook her head hard. "Be still."

All he heard was her gag and he let up a little. Then quickly before she recovered he stuffed his dick in her cunt. Dry, but the friction felt good. A cry of pain escaped her lips, but by then he had pinned her shoulders down and began to savor his entry. This bitch would know a real man had raped her when he finished with her this time.

"Raise your legs," he hissed at her, trying to probe deeper.

She obeyed, and he soon was pounding against her pubic bone. Not bad—no virgin, but he found her intriguing enough. He used one hand to raise her blouse, so by the starlight filtering in the window he could watch her large boobs shake with each poke.

He moved faster, she began to moan and it made him smile. Again he closed his hands around the smooth skin of her throat, then when he felt himself begin to come, he closed his fists tight on her windpipe, pressing his thumbs in on the serrations. In desperation, she bucked under him as his grip increased. Ready for his own pleasure, he drove his butt like a ram into her. Then he exploded inside with her back arched toward him, and he squeezed both hands harder and harder, feeling her windpipe collapse under his grip. Finally, she fell in a limp pile.

"Damn bitch," he swore. On all fours over her body, he considered doing it all over again to her. Fucking a dead woman was real fun while she was still warm. Once he'd tried to do it to a whore's corpse in a funeral home, but that one'd been dead for a day and her body was too cold to even enjoy doing it to her. Though he sent her to heaven with her full of his come. Better not do it to this one again—he shook his head in disappointment—because he still had the Flores woman to rape and kill that night as well.

His ear held close to her mouth, he could hear no breathing. She died easier than most, he decided, and wiped his slick dick off on her skirt, then he tossed the garment aside.

He glanced down in the starlight. Her bare legs spread apart, she was ready and waiting for him. He was encouraged to do it again to her, but he shook his head and reached for his pants on the floor. While getting dressed, he looked again with longing at her ghostly white form spread out on the pale sheet. Big waste not to do it once more to her; but in the end, he strapped on his gun and shrugged, ready to leave.

He promised himself he'd fuck that good-looking Flores woman once before she died and once afterward.

He slipped outside the woman's jackal, then he eased his way with careful stealth to the arroyo. He untied his horse's reins and with a grip of the large horn swung into the saddle. Pleased with himself, he booted the horse into a run and raced through the moonlight for Vaca and the Flores woman. One more bitch this night to rape and kill. He laughed aloud to himself.

6

Everyone in the party sworn to secrecy, they hurried back to the village. Best that they not be missed. Hernando was on his way to find the captain, and the women had swept all the telltale signs off the trail with boughs of juniper. Underneath the twinkling stars, Magdellania and Slocum walked leisurely back for her place.

"Your husband fought these bandits?" he asked as they moved in and out of the shadows cast by trees that loomed overhead.

"He lost his life fighting them."

"Shot down?"

"In the back."

"You know the killer?"

"It could only be one of Reyas's men." She turned away, obviously upset by the notion of the recall.

"Sorry," he said.

"Sorry—I can hardly speak of it—even now." She shook her head as if to escape the sorrow.

"But you feel certain that his men must have shot him?"

"Oh, yes. I suspected it was the red-headed one they call Durango."

"Why him?"

"He was in Vaca that night and he's a cold-blooded killer. He shot others down who had no guns."

"Was your husband armed?"

"Yes, but they shot him in the back."

"No chance, huh?"

"I hear a rider," she said and tugged him by the arm into the bushes. They stood in the darker shadows and watched the silhouette of a man slouched forward in the saddle, rushing by them on a hard-breathing horse.

"It's him. Durango," she hissed.

"Wonder what he's up to?" He looked off in the direction the man went, but saw nothing to indicate the rider's purpose in the night.

"No good, whatever it is," she said and they hurried for her place.

"We can have some sugared sopapillas—someone has been here." She sniffed as they entered her front door. "I can smell them."

He agreed with her as he noticed something fecal; his hand rested on his gun butt. The deep, musky aroma remained in the room like a night jar unemptied and about to overflow. Were the intruders still in there or close by?

"That damn Durango was here," she hissed.

"How do you know?"

"He's the only one smells that bad."

"What did he want?"

"What do you think?"

"Your guess. He ever been here before?"

"Once, but I ran him off with a pistol."

"Must have got his nerve back up again."

"Oh, Slocum, you don't even have a horse to get away from here. I feel I have jeopardized your life letting that boy take yours."

"Don't worry. We just need to sleep lighter and not in our beds."

"Good idea. I'll get some blankets and we can go out in back."

"Do you have a bell?"

"A bell?"

"Yes. Like a goat bell. We need to set up so if he returns the bell wakes us."

"Yes, I see. I have two in my cupboard. Copper bells."

"Wonderful. Do you have any yarn?"

"Yes."

Soon they had both doors set with the yarn stretched across them knee-high, alarmed with bells that would ring should anyone come through them. Then with her blankets over his shoulder, they went to the back of her flower garden and found a place to spread them out. Slocum wondered if she would stay close to him, but she obviously intended to keep her distance and spread hers a few feet away from his.

At last, bedded down, he removed the Colt from the holster to have it handy, grateful that he had not given it to Hernando. The night insects buzzed, and he used one arm for a pillow.

"Wake me if you hear the bells," he said and closed his eyes, ready for some sleep.

"I will," she promised and he went to sleep.

"Someone's at the casa," she whispered with her arm on his back to contain him.

"You hear the bells?" How long had he slept? No telling. It was still dark and he could hear someone cursing and a bell ringing. With his Colt in hand, he rose and headed for the dark square form of her jackal. Keeping low, he heard more furniture being kicked about.

"Gawdamn you, bitch, I know you're in here!" the party swore in Spanish. Dishes crashed. "I'm going to stick my dick down your throat!" the intruder raged. "Until you gag to death!"

Slocum reached the side window and pressed himself to the wall. Where was the madman? He listened and then decided he must be in the center of the room for he had overturned her table with another crash of more pottery.

Stepping to the opening, Slocum fired three quick shots with ear-shattering explosions and flashes of the muzzle, and he heard the party grunt like they were hit. Then, with Slocum's back pressed against the safety of the wall, the intruder opened fire at the window, emptying his pistol with a barrage of cuss words in both languages.

Slocum knew from the sounds the intruder was heading for the front door, so he started around the house to stop him. At the corner, a bullet chipped adobe dust that flew in his eyes, causing him to stop. Damn. He couldn't see enough to shoot for the grit in them. Then to his disgust, he heard the man whip his horse and race away in the night.

Opening and closing his eyelids to make them tear and flush out the grains in them, he leaned against the building as the hoofbeats faded into the night. His shoulder to the side of the building, he busied himself poking fresh ammo into the Colt until she arrived out of breath at his side.

"You hit?"

"No, a little crud in my eyes from where he shot at the wall is all."

"Let me look at them."

"I won't die, but I never got a good look at him."

"It was Durango. That stick-his-dick-in-my-mouth-till-he-chokes-me business. It was him."

"He needs to be taught some manners."

"Don't they all. Come inside, I want to look at your eyes."

"They'll be fine."

"Maybe so, after I look at them." She drew him by the arm inside the gun smoke–filled room.

He tried to see out of his blurred eyes. Impatience filled his mind; he had a score to settle with that bastard before he left this canyon.

She lighted a candle and he set the table upright. With a chair in the other hand for him, she seated him and began to look him over.

"Wonder you weren't shot," she said, wagging her head in disapproval. He noticed her honey-colored firm cleavage in his face as she examined his head for any wound. Too bad she was so set on being chaste; they could really warm up a pallet together. Lots of flesh under that flimsy cotton nightgown.

"What will we do now?" he asked.

"It isn't safe for you to stay here any longer."

"Then we must go into the mountains."

"I'll get some things that we can pack—"

His vision better, he busied himself being certain the Colt was reloaded. Satisfied, he holstered the weapon and looked around at all the destruction. Then he bent over, retrieved the first bell and pocketed it. They might need them again. Wouldn't hurt to have them.

In a short while, with sacks over their shoulders, she led him out the back way and they started up the steep canyon on foot. The starlight glinted like diamonds off the mica in the trail. The path was narrow and winding, and he soon found his breath short and they stopped to rest.

"It's another mile," she said. "But not so steep from there on."

"Good," he said with his hands on his knees, looking back in the dark abyss they left behind.

In the predawn, her leading the way, they reached some benchland. She pointed to a small wooden shack in a grove of pinyons. Part of some abandoned mine operation, he decided. The boards on the shacks were weathered a dull gray. He nodded his approval and she went ahead. Damn, where was his horse when he needed him—gone for help. He could only hope the young boy soon found the captain and returned with it.

She swept out the dust and then sprinkled the floor with water to keep the rest of the dust down. There were two bunks, a table, some crates for chairs and a dry sink. The windows were covered with translucent deerskin to let light in.

"How did this lumber get up here?"

"They cut and hand sawed it on the site," she said.

He nodded. It took a lot of work to saw out wood in a land where rock and adobe usually were the materials at hand. Then he noticed the sides were posts hewed and then put in the ground like a fort wall, with roof trusses on them and split shingles to make the roof. Still plenty of work.

"Was this mine very rich?"

"At one time, but they lost the vein."

"Happens to the best of them."

"Is this all right?" she asked.

He stepped over and swept her up in his arms and smiled into her face. "With you, Magdellania, I could stay on the moon."

The strength of her hands on his shoulders forced him to set her back down. Obviously she wanted no part of his advance—oh, well.

"This will be fine until the captain comes," he said, letting her go.

"Very good," she said, recovering her composure and straightening her skirt and blouse. When she looked up at last, the coldness was still in her eyes. So much for his trying.

7

"Only a flesh wound," Frio reported.

"Ah, Durango will live then," Reyas said to him. He rose from his desk and walked to the window. That Flores woman must have shot him. They already reported from the village that the bitch Raverez had been found dead in her bed. Amused, Reyas smiled to himself. Being shot was what Durango deserved for trying to kill two women on the same night. An image of the straight-backed Flores woman brought a smile to his face. That *puta* was perhaps a black widow who killed those that tried to mate with her. This time she only wounded the filthy one.

A picture of her haughty ways only intrigued him more. The stupid ones he sent to arrest her husband got scared and shot him instead. Otherwise, she would already have been under his power. Durango was one of those he sent, though he denied it was his bullet—ah, but it was always hard to control such a rabid dog from biting too much. But the señora—he shook his head to dismiss his erotic thoughts about her. He needed to plan how to leave this place in case the Ruralists came. Debrewski was unbribable—others had tried and lost—but so far the man had not ventured into these parts of the Sierra Madras.

Why did the captain send such a gringo for a scout? Easy enough, he was a tough one. He would have sent such an *hombre* had he been seeking information. How much time did he have left? Two more burro trains were ready to leave the canyon loaded with high-grade ore. One should start for New Mexico on the hour.

He had enough money in the Silver City bank to live a good life, but he might need more. Once he left this place, he could never return, even with an army of *pistoleros*, and retake it. The only way was to grab the best of it while he could and get out before the Ruralists arrived. He needed to send his three prized stallions to Silver City in the morning too. They would be the basis for his horse breeding business. Even as he planned his final days, he could visualize his life as a rich *patrón* in New Mexico. There would be carriages, social events, and he would need to find a woman like Señora Flores to accompany him, perhaps even to attend the governor's ball in Sante Fe. Perhaps a second house there too. Oh, it must be a grand one.

"Señor?" someone called out and broke into his daydreaming.

He turned and frowned as his men Torga and Manuel rushed into his office.

"What's wrong now?" he demanded.

"When the men went to relieve them, they found the guards at the south canyon had been murdered."

"Killed them? Who killed them?" He felt an arrow in his chest.

"There are no tracks. They swept them away. The three guards are dead with no wounds."

His lips pursed tight, he tried to think who would do such a thing. Then the notion struck him. That scout must have killed them, so he could get back to Debrewski. Damn, things grew worse by the minute. "Where's that gringo calls himself Slocum?"

The henchmen shook their heads with no answer. Then

Torga spoke: "We also saw there was a fight last night at the Flores house, but the scout, Slocum, and his horse are not there. The widow and him, they vamoose."

"Did they go out the south way?"

"*Patrón,* the tracks were swept clean. We don't know."

"Go the village and find out who rode away last night. Torture a few until they tell you. We should have shot that Slocum, scout or no scout." He clenched his fists at his side and studied the underside of the ceiling for some form of celestial help. An uncomfortable pressure grew inside his chest that shortened his wind, and his left arm ached.

"*Patrón,* what should we do about the guard post?"

"Get two men you can trust and put them down there. Tell them it pays double, but warn them that those crazy people in Vaca might get them too if they leave their guard down."

Manuel nodded. "Strange thing, *Patrón,* when we found Juan he died with his pants down."

"No wounds?" Reyas squeezed his whiskered chin and paced the room.

"None on them. They were lying around dead."

"In that village, someone knows how they died. They also know where that Slocum and the widow are at."

"What should we do when we find them?"

"Bring them here, of course. And Manuel—"

"*Si, Patrón.*"

"If any of those guards hear any word of the Ruralists coming here, they are to report at once to me."

"*Si, Patrón.*"

When both men left the office and he could see from the window they had mounted their horses for the return trip to Vaca, he turned to his clerk. "Send the stable man Francisco to see me."

He needed to get those stallions on their way. This Slocum gone and his guards dead from whatever meant that the time he must leave drew even closer. Seated at the desk, he looked up when the horse handler entered.

"Francisco, I want to send the three stallions to Silver City and begin the breeding program up there. We can do more business selling high-price horses and find the mares we need up there."

The thin man with the black mustache agreed with a sharp nod. Francisco never said much, but he knew horses and Reyas felt certain he was the right man for this operation.

"You must start at once for there. My banker, Señor Cartwright, in Silver City will find you a place to stable them. I shall send a letter with you and the money you will need, of course."

"How many men should I take?"

"How many do you need?"

"Two?"

"Fine. When you are ready to leave, come by and Alphanso will have the letter for the banker and your money."

Francisco nodded and left the room.

"Write Señor Cartwright—" he said aloud to his clerk in the outer office.

"I am already preparing it."

"Good." The boy was very efficient. Since Reyas could not even read or write himself, having Alphanso to do such tasks was necessary. Had the young clerk's balls even dropped? He doubted it. Perhaps he was sixteen or so—nothing like Reyas had been at that age. He had a hard-on all the time from fourteen on—God forgive him, but the sheep bleated and ran away when he came upon them. The mare donkeys all brayed in protest at his approach. Young women giggled and blushed when he went past them—*grande* was the word for the size of his manhood. *Muy grande*.

"I'm going to the mine," he said over his shoulder to his clerk and ducked out the open door. The climb to the entrance was always breathtaking up the wide path that wound to where the great vagina-like opening gaped between the folds of the towering cliffs. This time his chest felt different and more than being out of wind from the climb too.

The superintendent, Rudy, met him. His face covered in dust, he led Reyas aside from the cart traffic that rumbled along on the wooden rails to deliver the ore and the rock waste to the entrance.

"How are you coming?" Reyas asked him.

"We found a new rich pocket this morning."

"Ah, how rich?"

"High-grade stuff."

"Good. Can you work them any harder?"

Rudy shook his head and removed his pith helmet. "No, they won't last. Besides we are getting out all you can pack train out."

"You've heard the Ruralists may come," Reyas said behind his hand.

The man acknowledged his words.

"You may take the last burro load of ore for yourself."

The man nodded he had heard him.

"Make it a rich one. You have been very loyal to me. Your work in the mine here has been important. May we both be rich forever. Tell no one."

"I won't. How much time do we have?" The man frowned, his dust-floured face looking perplexed.

"I fear only days."

"I will be ready and I'll take the back way out."

Reyas heard him and nodded. "Later, you must come see me at my casa at Silver City?"

"Certainly."

Then Reyas smiled at his man, pleased at the notion in the future they might be partners again. "We may find a mine up there."

"Exactly."

Outside in the sunshine, he looked over the ore dumped on the ground for repacking. Grayish-looking rocks, nothing like gold, the value of which you could tell upon simple examination. He could hardly distinguish silver in the ore form from worthless rocks. Workers on their knees nodded to him as they packed the precious rocks in canvas panniers.

Such a shame, he thought as he looked off across the canyon as more slag was dumped on the growing pile, to simply leave such a rich mine. A few more years and he would have had money enough to have bought railroad companies in the U.S. or even Mexico. He could have been a great baron of industry—oh, well, he had enough in the Silver City bank according to that boy, Alphanso, to live well forever.

Good boy. He must find out if he ever bedded a woman. That might be his present to the faithful clerk, a sex slave. Oh, he could have worn out two such women when he was at that age.

What killed those three guards bothered him. No marks on them. Only poison could do that. Manuel and Torga would learn the names of the responsible ones—they'd torture enough of them they'd find out the truth. Stupid peons in Vaca. There was always work at the mine; he paid his workers well. No, they were all rebels, farmers and cattlemen. Of course, he needed their crops and meat to feed his workers. Still they had cut the throats of two of his best *pistoleros* while they had lain drunk upon the ground.

Perhaps he should have gotten stricter with them over that incident. Now they had killed three more and wiped out the tracks—was that gringo Slocum that they could not find behind all of this? Perhaps.

Reyas wandered in the office and nodded to the boy when he looked up.

"The letter to the banker is complete, and I have put a hundred pesos in the purse for Francisco."

"Very good; go and have your lunch now and take a siesta. You are my best man, Alphanso."

"Gracias, Patrón."

"We must begin to bag what we need to take. I fear soon we too must leave this place. Order some panniers for the things we must take."

"Oh, we can put the necessary things on one mule," the boy advised him.

"Very good. Pick a sound one that won't spook and jump off the trail."

"I will, *Patrón*."

"Gracias."

The slight youth put on his hat and disappeared out the doorway with a quick good-bye. Reyas watched him hurry off. He noticed the boy talk to some young, attractive girls

on their way to get water. Then his clerk disappeared from
sight among the village jackals; Reyas looked off down the
trail to Vaca. Perhaps he would go to his own quarters and
have some food and wine. What woman would share his
bed? No sign of that girl Annette, his men had done that
right anyway. Perhaps he would screw Felicia, the short one
who giggled—ah, no mind, he set out for his casa.

He entered the door and his cook, Rosa, looked up from
the hearth. A thickset woman, she did the cooking and he
could see she was busy at the fireplace.

"*Cabrito?*" she asked as the griddle sizzled and browned
vegetables and meat.

"*Si.*" Her milk-fat kid meat would be good. Rosa knew
how to butcher goats. Never did she get any hair on the meat
nor did they ever taste fecal. Her thin-bladed knife slipped
under the hide and cut outward so no split hairs were ever
on the carcass.

He took his place at the head of the wooden table. She
came over and poured wine for him in a glass. "It will be
ready in a few minutes."

He nodded and sipped the wine in his crystal glass. Perhaps he should give a reward for that gringo's head. That
might be better than torture—honey worked faster than vin-
egar. If his first plan did not work, then the reward—yes,
that would make them find him. When he finished his lunch,
he'd go by Alphanso's jackal and get him to undo the safe
so he could get out enough pesos to buy Slocum's head.

Full and feeling content, he left his casa and picked his
teeth with a sharpened stick. Alphanso lived up the hill a
ways and the sun grew hotter. He passed several women that
he considered taking to their casa and romping with. Already
at the hovel where his clerk lived, he started up the bank for
the front door. He could hear some heavy breathing and loud
grunting, and a smile broke out. Sounded as if his boy had
found him one.

He slowed down so he could peek in on this affair. When
he could look around the corner, he saw the boy's snowy
hatchet ass and skinny legs with his scrotum swinging wildly

between them and him humping away on top of the girl on all fours. My, such fun—then Reyas blinked in disbelief. That wasn't a girl. He could see Alphanso was reaching around and jacking off the hard dick of some boy underneath him. The sounds of their pleasure turned his stomach over.

Mother of God! His clerk was a faggot. A homosexual. Their grunting, jacking off and coupling made him nauseated; he wished to drive the sight from his mind. He shook his head and turned away, ready to vomit. How many times had he wanted a son just like his clerk? A son like that. Oh, God, the whole thing made him upset. Stunned, he went back to the office and collapsed in his chair. What should he do next? Nothing for the moment—he needed that boy's skills too badly to do a single thing. But in time he would eliminate him—he shuddered all over in revulsion at the thought of his skinny clerk corn holing that other boy.

The picture of the two boys in action would not leave his mind. He poured himself a glass of mescal and hoped to wash it away. Three glasses later, nothing helped.

8

"They are torturing the Mendozas," the girl of sixteen said in a whisper. Her face ashen white and gasping for her breath, she drew in deep gulps of air. "I have tried to find you for hours."

"Seriously torturing them?" Slocum asked.

"They have them naked, hanging by their thumbs."

"That's serious."

"Wait," Magdellania said, capturing his sleeve when he started to leave. "It's a trap."

"What're they asking them?" Slocum asked the girl.

"Where is the gringo? Who poisoned the guards at the south end of the canyon?"

Slocum exchanged a head shake with Magdellania. "I better go try to help them."

"Sure, and you get yourself killed?"

"The villagers won't stop them. Those men did nothing to deserve that kind of treatment."

"How will you stop them?"

"Where do they have them strung up at?"

"Near the cantina. But they say they will torture more of us if they do not talk."

"Can I get close to the cantina and they not see me?"

The pale-faced young girl nodded. "You can come up the arroyo behind. There is much brush to cover you coming that way."

"Take an hour or longer," Magdellania complained. "They may have killed them by then."

"Chance we need to take." Slocum considered that all he had was one pistol. If he came across the river in the open, they'd certainly see him long before the Colt was effective. "How else can I get close faster?"

"Dressed as woman with other women in a mob. They would never suspect you are there," Magdellania said.

"Too dangerous."

"When you are dead and gone, what will those bastards do to us? Rape and kill us. We must end their reign of terror. And eliminate all of his men—Reyas too."

"I'm game, but if the shooting starts—" He shook his head. "What if someone warns them I'm coming."

"We will cut their tongue out for an example."

He blinked at her. Certainly she had changed her ways. Before she didn't want them killed, now she wanted their confederates speechless.

"What are you thinking?" he finally asked.

"I think we must rid this place of the vermin, whether Captain Debrewski comes or not."

"Donna," he said to the girl. "Get the women that you can trust. Have them dress in black as if they all were going to a funeral and we will march over there, praying on beads and wailing a lot."

"I can do that. But clothes for him?" She looked at Magdellania.

"I can dress him well enough under a black scarf and blanket; they will think he's another mourner too.

"I will gather them and we will be ready to cross the river when you get there."

"Good," Magdellania said and began to go through her things they brought to the cabin.

Donna left on the run and Slocum picked up a dark blanket and wrapped himself in it. "How do I look?"

She came with a black scarf and tied his head up. When she stood back she nodded in approval. "You can pass at a distance for a woman, but you must walk bent over. You're too tall."

"I can even do that."

"If we only can get you close enough to get the drop on them—"

He agreed. "Then I'll handle the rest."

She looked to be certain the girl was gone and turned to him. "When this is over, I want you." She reached out and touched his chest with her fingertips. "To teach me how to make love again."

He nodded he heard her.

They hurried off the mountain. No sign of Donna ahead of them; the poor girl must have ran all the way back to Vaca. He carried the blanket and shawl over his arm—their plan needed to work so no one got hurt. Hiding behind the skirts of women was not his style, but no way he could cross the river and the open space to the cantina and not alert Reyas's men in the process.

When they reached Magdellania's yard, a number of women in black were already there and others came, changing to dark clothes, so they numbered well over a dozen. They didn't seem to care he was there; they removed their work dress and skirts and put on the black ones. It was "moon Slocum" day in her yard as they hurriedly dressed and Magdellania re-explained the plan to them.

A middle-aged woman with a dark shadow of a mustache on her upper lip held her arms up and called for their attention. "Anyone tries to warn those two *bastardos* will get my stiletto in their kidneys. Do you understand?"

The nods and searching of each other's faces were apparent. He let Magdellania fit the shawl on his head and tie it. Hot thing to wear, he decided. Other women came and they too changed among the crowd.

"Lupe will lead us. Crowd around Slocum, so they can't

see him. If you can't wail, do Hail Marys. We must all clear
the way when he is ready to draw his gun on them." Magdellania nodded to him. "You better wear sandals, those
boots are too obvious. Besides we must ford the river."

He agreed and kicked them off, taking the footwear that
she handed him. A couple of women steadied him as he bent
over to put them on each foot. She gave him a pensive pose
to her lips. He shrugged as if he couldn't help that they
wanted to assist him.

So the mob of wailing and praying women began down
the trail for the river. Bent over and moving with them, he
wished for another revolver, but his own with five loads in
the cylinder would have to be enough. Two men were all
they said were at the cantina. How many locals would go to
the bandits' aid when he tried to get the drop on them? No
one knew for certain, so he didn't bother to ask. Always
some traitors lurked in the side wings; this day they might
show their hands. Just so none of these brave women with
him were harmed.

Ahead was the river, out of the shade in the glaring sun,
and he could barely make out the top of the cantina building
across the silver water. Magdellania held his left arm and
guided him. With his head so bowed, it was hard to see much
unless he straightened. This was some march.

They crossed the cold river in a tight group, wailing and
praying en masse. He felt relieved when they made the far
side—his feet felt like ice cubes and his pants were wet to
the knees, the water adding to the weight of the blanket he
hugged tight at his throat.

"What the hell are you doing?" one of Reyas's men
shouted at them.

"That was Torga," Magdellania said, close to his ears over
the wailing of the others. "Manuel is closer to the tree where
the boys are."

"How far apart are they?"

"A ways," she said, sounding disappointed.

"Keep going closer," he said, not daring to even look up.

"To the tree," one woman ordered and the mass flowed that direction.

"I say stop!" Torga ordered. Then Slocum could hear the ring of his spur rowels as he ran to head them off.

"Good, he's going to join his partner," she told him.

He changed hands on the blanket and drew his Colt. It was hot under the damn thing and all he could see were black skirts that flowed around him.

"Halt there!" a woman's voice said. "We need to talk to you. These men you hold are our children."

"Tell us what we want to know and they can go free." The tone of the man's voice did not sound certain.

Magdellania took a better hold on his arm. The others still wailed as she began to guide him closer to the front, women parting for his passage.

"They put away their guns," she hissed.

"Good."

"Tell us who killed the guards and these two can go or else—"

"We are poor people, but can we offer you gold?" the woman pleaded.

"No—no, we need the truth about those men who died."

"How much gold will you take to stop the torture?" she insisted over the cries that continued in wake fashion.

"No, we can't take gold."

Slocum was near the front of the crowd, still bent over and seeing that his line of fire would not endanger the two naked men hanging to the left. Good, time for action.

"Then get your hands up or die," he shouted, straightening and tossing off the blanket.

The wailing stopped and only the rush of the river could be heard. A mockingbird sounded off. He ripped the scarf aside. Ready, he waited with the hammer cocked for their response.

"How did you—"

"Raise your hands or go for your guns," Slocum reiterated.

The seconds ticked. The fatter-faced one acted undecided, then slowly he raised his hands. The mustache woman charged in and, assisted by others, they disarmed them. A shout went up and the women rushed over to the prisoners. There were two on each of the boys' legs holding them up while a nimble woman scrambled up the tree and slashed the ropes. Freed, the two young men were hugged by many and their thumbs examined by the concerned. Soon wrapped in blankets, they were hurried to the shade.

The two henchmen were bound and tied feet and hands by the zealous posse members. Slocum holstered his own Colt and picked up theirs. They had three pistols and more ammo. One of the women returned with their horses and he added the two breech-loading rifles in their scabbards and forty rounds of ammo to his arsenal.

"What now?" Magdellania asked as a young girl brought him his boots.

Seated on the ground, he brushed off his soles. "Take out the guards at each post. Then he won't have anyone behind our backs when we take on the mine."

"You aren't going to wait for Debrewski?" With her left eye closed, she squinted against the high sun's glare at him.

"If he even comes. No, we need to arm the men that we can and take the mine."

"We don't need to arm the men," the mustache lady said. "Give us women the weapons; we will clean them out."

"Canyon guards first. Maybe you women can captivate them into surrendering." Slocum shook his head and accepted her hand to help him up. Stomping on his boots, he considered the crowd of serious faces around him.

"Who will guard the prisoners?" he asked.

"We will put them in the cantina and they better not get away," the mustache lady said clear enough even Slocum felt the threat.

He wanted to laugh as the two thrust-up men were carried inside the cantina and left. The women came out clapping their hands. The mustache lady put her head in past the doors and shouted her words at whoever was inside. "They better be here when we get back!"

"That's Ronica," Magdellania said.

"She ain't taking no for an answer either," Slocum said amused at her forceful ways.

"How do we take them?" a woman asked.

"There must be new guards on the river outlet."

"Yes, Manuel and Torga took two new ones down there."

"They will be suspicious."

"Not of some drunk women," one said. "I will get a guitar and a few of us will stroll down there like we are very drunk. They will think it is party time. Then we will whack them over the head."

"Be careful, they must know what happened to the last three."

"We can do it." She curled her lip. "They all got hard peters to rule them."

"Yes," went up the agreement. One woman ran in the cantina and came out with a guitar. Armed with her instrument, the crowd crossed the stream again. Slocum rode one of the henchmen's horses and led the other.

They were singing a song about a wild horse that got away. He enjoyed their music. In a short while, they grew quiet as they approached the guards and three of the prettier girls were chosen, plus the older woman who played the guitar. Slocum took one of the rifles from the women in case there was a need.

Down the trail went the singers, sounding a little drunk and the girls prancing and dancing their way while Mama strummed the guitar. Slocum and Magdellania went through the brush until they could view the pair of guards from seclusion. He liked the shocked look on the two men's faces when the silly girls came prancing into their view. They rose with rifles in hand. At that point, one of the girls ran over and took one of their hats off their head. She flung it on the ground and, like a free spirit, raised her skirt shamelessly while she danced around it.

Slocum nodded at Magdellania. The guard put his rifle down and began to dance with her. He squeezed her hard to him and they went round and round to the music. Another girl approached the second man. He shook his head and held the rifle closer. Soon she was standing before him laughing and she reached out and cupped his crotch in her hand. He stopped backing up and stood there as if frozen. Slocum could almost read the words on her lips. She jerked his belt open and his pants fell. He never moved when she stepped in closer and took a hold to begin jacking him off. He set the rifle on its butt and soon he threw his head back in pleasure and the carbine fell to the ground. That was when Ronica hit him over the head with a rock and they also took out the dancer.

The pair was quickly tied and both unceremoniously loaded belly down across the horse and taken back to the cantina. His posse was beginning to show pride in their work. The entourage left the "jail" that held four prisoners and started up the trail that Slocum came in on. On the left fork, they found the guards taking a nap. Without a struggle, they were "arrested" and soon joined the others in the tied position upon the cantina floor.

"Is anyone else down here?" Slocum asked.

"I will ask that pig, Manuel," Ronica said and went back inside.

In a few minutes she returned. "He wasn't going to tell me. So I kicked him in the *huevos* a couple of times." The laughter and cheers of approval went up from the women at the notion of how Manuel's balls had been attacked. "He swears no one else is down here."

"There's no one?"

"None." The woman shook her head as if satisfied. "How do we take the mine?"

"We first must get all the women and children out of the village up there, so none will get hurt. You can do it a few at a time. When we have them all safely out, then we will take the office and after that the mine."

"What if Reyas catches us taking the women out?"

"Then we change plans."

They nodded.

"Who knows some of the women well enough to make them come out peacefully?" he asked the posse.

"My cousin will come."

Another woman waved. "I have friends living there who hate Reyas."

"Good, you two go in first and lead them out. Don't bring them out by the trail, someone will see you. Go out through the woods so he doesn't see anything."

They nodded and filed into the timber to stay out of sight.

"I will go back to my casa and some of us will cook food for everyone," Magdellania said.

"Be careful," he said to them as they headed for the mine. "If my plan works, in a few hours, we should have this job completed."

She leaned over and kissed him on the mouth. "*Gracias*, this is going so well."

He drew a sharp breath and nodded. Whew, he was ready. Another woman came and explained her cousin would come out. He told her to go ahead with the others, but to be careful.

9

Durango heard the women talking in the other room. Despite the hurting in his side, he sat up on the palette and crawled closer to the door to listen.

"You must come at once. They have taken all the guards prisoner, including Manuel and Torga and they will take Reyas and the rest soon."

"How many men do they have?" the woman whispered.

"They have plenty plus many guns and pistols. But they don't want the women and children hurt in case there is a fight."

"But what if—"

"Don't worry—get the children and come on."

"But—"

"No. You must come quickly."

He knew enough. Filled with the urgency to get out of there, he stood with a twinge of pain in his side and crossed the room, scooping up his gun holster. In a minute, he went out the window. Ducking low, he headed for the corrals. They weren't taking him. No time to warn anyone or draw any of his money, damn. Reyas owed him three months' pay. He found a good roan in the pen and caught him. What if he went around them? Go out through the opposite side to the river and they would never see him.

Searching around and observing nothing, he threw the saddle on one-handed and soon had the roan cinched. He might need a second horse. Unseen fingers crawled up the skin on the back of his neck when he went for another animal. His guts crawled with anticipation as he saddled an extra bay horse. His adrenaline had made the wound stop hurting. Mounted on the roan, he started around the pens, leading the bay. He went behind the offices and warehouse and splashed off into the feeder stream fed by a huge spring. Up the far bank he rode, feeling grateful that all the washwomen were taking siestas or fleeing to the woods—it suited him that no one saw his escape.

Sticking close to the far side of the stream and behind the brush, he hoped not to be seen by any of this oncoming army of invaders. Halfway to Vaca, he felt better, but remained on the far side until he dared come out. Glancing over his shoulder, he rode the roan at a trot, ready to flee at the first sign of this army.

He reined up short. Was the widow Flores at home? It might sweeten the ride if he had her along. Bad enough that Reyas owed him all that money he would never collect.

The horses tied to bushes, he went to the edge of the brush and spied up and down the river. The crossing here in the narrows he knew would be treacherous and deep; still, if he forded lower down, they might have lookouts. With no one in sight, he went back and recovered his animals. Forced to spur the roan off the bank into the churning water, the horse soon began to swim. One-handed, he clung to the horn, his other arm about jerked off by the second horse's hesitation.

Frightened by the force of the water once in the current, the bay scrambled to keep his head out of the water. Washed downstream, Durango wondered how stupid his idea to cross there had been and if he would make it. A sharp pain in his side from the wound, he swallowed mouthfuls of the cold water and wondered if the struggling roan would ever find any footing. At last, he was forced to release the bay. The brown horse, so frantic with fear, kept rising up as if to walk on the surging surface.

Swept away from the bank twice, the roan at last swam in where his hooves were on solid bottom and lunged up a steep bank. Durango clung to the saddle horn, not daring to lose him. Then with an ear-shattering scream, the roan lost his footing and fell over backward off the slope. The crash into the water put Durango under. Swallowing water, he found himself submerged beneath the desperate animal, fighting for his own life. His breath gone with the first mouthful, he fought for consciousness and tried to swim for the surface with his arms. His sodden boots were like lead weights. He could see the sun shining on the surface, but the swift current swept him away from his goal.

At last, he crawled out on a sandy beach, puking water and sourness and gripping his wounded side. After fainting, he came to, spitting sand from his mouth, and fought his way to his knees. The burning in his side was so pain filled he could only curl up and cuss Slocum as he hugged himself to stop the hurting.

He had no way to know how long he had lain on the ground. Finally he mustered enough strength to get to his feet. His feet sloshing in his water-filled boots and his clothing plastered to his skin, he managed to find the bay. Mounted at last, he bent over the saddle in discomfort from the wound knifing him, then rode downstream searching for the roan. He'd need the extra horse to kidnap her. *Those bastards would pay for this—especially that Slocum sumbitch.*

He emerged through some willows and spotted the downcast roan. The dark saddle was still on him—good. He searched around. No one in sight. So far he hadn't attracted any attention. Best get her and ride the hell out, then he could figure out what he needed to do. Reyas owed him money—lots of it. Someday, he'd collect that up in the States. That pimple-faced faggot of a clerk, Alphanso, had told him all about the Silver City bank after he'd put the edge of his big knife to that little queer's scrotum.

The recall of that boy's fear-filled face and huge eyes brought a chuckle out of Durango. He wrinkled his nose— poking boys in the butt never did interest him much, but that time he had a mission. He wondered for a long time where Reyas kept all his money, so honeying up to the kid was all in his plan. When he got the kid undressed and all fired up, instead of giving that flush-faced pervert what he expected, Durango grabbed him by his pecker, jerked him up close and laid the knife's edge to his sack. In a second, he had all the answers he wanted about Reyas's banking.

Durango couldn't see anyone in sight, so he booted the bay out on the road, leading the roan, and headed for the widow's place. She'd entertain him for a while. Give Reyas time to get all set up in Silver City and he'd ride in there and collect double what the bastard owed him.

From the cover of brush, he studied her jackal. He wondered if Slocum was around. He shifted the Colt on his hip, thank God he hadn't lost it in the dunking. Dismounted, his spur rowels jingled and the water squished between his toes as he made his way stealthily to the side of the adobe shack. Where would she be?

Then he heard horses and quickly retreated to the back of the building. He could hear her voice, and the image of her long, pointed breasts made his water-shriveled privates crawl. Who was with her? He couldn't see the other person, but it wasn't Slocum.

"We'll need food for them," Magdellania said and he heard another woman answer. He sure didn't need two of them. Another time, he'd take both of them—but he wasn't certain how much time he dared to dally around there. Better kill the other one.

Both women were talking. He bent over and went underneath the window, straightened to his full height beside the door facing. Better shoot the second one—he drew the Colt, stepped in the doorway, and when he spotted the girl of perhaps seventeen, he cocked the hammer, aimed and squeezed the trigger. The hammer snapped on a dud.

The girl screamed and out of nowhere Magdellania struck

him over the head with an iron pot. The blow addled him and he took a second try to shoot the hysterical girl. That one snapped too.

"Run, Rosita! Tell Slocum to come fast," Magdellania shouted and hit him over the head again with the iron pot. His knees buckled. He managed to cock the Colt again. That shot went into the floor. Billowing dust and gun smoke filled the air as his world spun around. She struck him a third time and the lights went out.

He awoke and spit dirt from his mouth. Facedown, his hands tied behind his back, he wondered where the two women were at. Straining at his binds that also held his feet together, the hemp cut deep into his wrists. No time for pain—he had to get loose or his life wasn't worth ten centavos. Damn that bitch!

"Ride, Rosita. But tell Slocum that I have that evil one bound and tied and not to come back until he has the mine business settled. I will be fine here."

"But—"

"Ride, we can fix food later."

By the clatter of hooves he knew the girl was gone. Had the ropes given any? He was uncertain of any progress, belly down, his cheek resting on the gritty floor. She would pay for this when he got loose. He strained even harder to free himself, then stopped when he heard her sandals approaching.

"Did you kill my husband?" she asked, from the safety of a few feet.

"What was his name?" he asked, acting dumb.

"No, you knew him. He knew you too and you spoke to him by name once. I can recall that."

"I know lots of people—I can't remember."

"When Slocum gets here, your mind will be better," she said and swished past.

"What are they doing up there?"

"Liberating the mine."

"Oh, I see. Who will take Reyas's place then, Slocum?"

"He says it can be a co-op, belong to all the workers."

"Generous of him. You pay him enough money, he'll do that."

"What do you know? You rape women and children, murder people like my husband." She spat at him.

He wanted to laugh; he'd teach her better respect when he got loose. Time was what bothered him, he didn't have much of that left. Then the rope gave a little and restored his faith. Maybe, maybe he had some slack. Careful not to work it when he felt she was looking at him, he raised his head to locate her. Nowhere in sight, she must have gone after something. He gave a Herculean strain, tearing his own flesh on the rough rope, and managed to loosen his hands.

Once more he checked for her. No sign, so he rolled over and drew a smaller knife from his boot top and severed the ropes on his legs. In haste, he rose to his feet and tried to shake the pounding in his head—then footsteps alerted him.

She was coming back. His breath caught, and he stepped aside and pressed his back to the wall. When she entered, he threw his arm around her and pointed the knife tip at her face.

"I'll cut off your nose like some damn Apache squaw," he hissed in her ear.

Her resistance stopped.

"Better," he whispered in her ear and with a fistful of her hair he shoved her ahead. "You've got three minutes to get your shit in a sack and get ready to ride out of here with me."

"Never—"

His backhanded slap to her face spun her around. She caught herself on the dry sink. The empty dishpan she upset spun around and crashed on the floor.

"You can go with your things or without—you got any damn cartridges?" He searched around. Had to reload his handgun—those in it were too wet. Hell's bells, what else would go wrong? He dumped the cartridges from his pistol out on his wet boot toes.

"I'll pack—no ammo—I'll—" She staggered away, acting

disoriented and holding the side of her face that he had struck.

Good—he had her under his power. Since she'd told that other bitch for Slocum not to hurry back, the two of them should get far away before Slocum even knew about her being kidnapped. His plan would work—despite all of his problems. The water in his boots still angered him, but they would dry. More concerned about her actions, he watched her stuff some clothing in a sack. Good—they could leave in a minute. When he finally got dried out . . . visions of him using her willowy body brought a smile to his thick lips. She would know he was stud—but he could hardly contain himself thinking about how sweet her ass would be. For him.

He loaded her on the bay and fixed a riata for a lead, then he mounted the roan. In the saddle, he studied her as she looked expectantly toward the mine. Wiping his upper lip on the side of his hand, he wanted to tell her to forget Slocum—he'd never find them. Then he jerked the bay's lead.

"Hang on or fall off," he shouted and set spurs to the roan. They left out in a hard run for the south.

10

Reyas spotted them coming at the edge of the clearing and frowned at what he saw. Why all the gawdamn women? Armed too. He turned back to Alphanso, who was clearing out the safe.

"Get that money and get out of here. They're almost here."

The wide-eyed boy dropped a stack of bills and they fluttered to the floor. Reyas saw them and then frowned as the clerk scrambled to pick them up. The loose money gave him an idea.

"We don't have time for that. Go, the horses wait!" he shouted, catching a sight of the female army advancing into the clearing.

"But the money—"

"Never mind, I say, get out back and give me a lot of that paper money." He began putting stacks inside his shirt and shoved the boy toward the back door. "Go. Your life's worth more than a few dollars."

Alphanso rushed out and Reyas ducked to look out the front window at the advance of the women—damn, he could see they had rifles. He took his knife and slit two canvas bags of coins and strew them over the office. Then he rushed outside the back door and mounted the powerful gray. The boy was already headed into the pines—good. Those women on foot would be no match for their horses. He spurred the gray after the boy for the timber.

When he reached the first high spot, he pulled out a stack of paper currency and began to toss it away. It was crazy of him throwing away hundreds of dollars—but when those whores saw all that currency they would stop and gather it.

"Patrón—" Alphanso asked, coming back, dismayed at his money scattering.

"I am buying off the posse. Throw a sack of gold coins down, but scatter it. We want them all to have a chance to stop and pick it up." Reyas pulled out another stack of bills and added them to the pine needle litter. He rode his gray in circles dealing out the paper.

Laughing at the top of his voice, he spurred the gray about through the pines, spreading his wealth. Soon he shouted to the boy that it was time for them to leave. They both sent their horses up the mountain on the fly. By nightfall, Reyas planned to be over the mountain, and in four days, in Demming, far beyond the Ruralists or any stupid pursuers.

That evening he and his clerk dined on *pulcia* boiled in their tin cups on the small fire. The sweet mixture of corn-meal and brown sugar carried in leather bags was sustaining and the ration that was carried by most vaqueros. It would not spoil in the heat, was easy to fix and furnished a lot of energy, plus the sweetness satisfied the person's appetite.

Reyas sprawled on his side and considered the small tongues of blue flame that licked at the darkness. The notion struck him that the boy he had so long trusted was a bugger of men. He closed his eyes; for years he knew someday this would happen—he would be forced from the mine. His reign had lasted over seven years, a long time, and he about over-stayed his place. All this money in the New Mexico bank would be enough—still, he must not show the boy his dis-approval for he needed him until . . .

Absently, he tossed some twigs in the fire and on the coals; they surged up into yellow flares. A new clerk would be the answer, but he must be careful. In Silver City, he would hire a gringo and let Alphanso train him. Then one night when his apprentice was well trained, he would cut the faggot's throat and bury him out of sight. The very notion he was sharing camp with such an abomination made him shudder in disgust.

"This banker's name is Cartwright?" he asked absently.

"Thurman Cartwright."

"Good," he said and sprawled on his back to look at the sky full of stars and wonder what was happening at the mine.

"Money," screamed the woman who rushed out of the office holding fistfuls.

The word went up from the assembled females and the stampede was on for the office door. Slocum hurried around back and thought he saw a gray horse entering the stand of pines up the slope. From the sounds in the office, he decided money must be spilled all over. He bent over and retrieved a few ten-dollar bills. It covered the floor like fall leaves.

"Señor? Señor?" He looked around to see who was calling to him and ran to the front door through all the bent-over women picking up loot. The young woman who had left earlier with Magdellania to secure some food for the posse came charging on horseback up to the office.

"Rosita, what is wrong?" He caught her lathered horse and held him for her as she dismounted in a flurry of white petticoats.

"Magdellania has captured the murderer Durango and has him tied up at her casa."

"She all right?" He glanced down the canyon at the cottonwoods that marked the trail head to the village.

"Yes. She hit him many times over the head with an iron pot, then we tied his hands and feet."

"You're certain?"

"Si. She said for you not to worry, but do what you needed to do up here."

"I reckon that mine's next." He glanced skyward and frowned as he saw several miners on the ridge. They dumped off two bodies that bounced headfirst over the slag pile. When they came to rest, Slocum could see he did not recognize either of them. Must have been Reyas's mine bosses. He looked again as the men on top shouted over their success.

Looked like their bondage to Reyas was over. The miners ran for the trail that came down the steep mountain and women with fistfuls of money screamed for them to hurry. Slocum tucked his portion of the find in his shirt pocket and went for his horse. Reyas had a good head start, but going after them was a matter of riding down the tracks until he found his quarry.

"Señor Slocum?" A breathless middle-aged woman ran over, shaking her head to dismiss something. "Reyas's gone. We won't let him come back. Stay and help us set up this mine so we all can prosper."

"Democracies are very fragile," he said, reining up the horse.

"Yes, but if you ever have freedom, you can hardly stand the taste of a dictator."

He nodded as he considered the low education and knowledge of the men and women of the village. Someone else would probably prey on them—he glanced at the mountain, longing to go after the deposed ruler, but in the end, he surrendered and agreed to her insistence to remain there and help the people.

In the office, he smiled at the woman who held up a gold coin she found beneath the counter. He looked at the letterhead on a paper on the floor—Thurman Cartwright, President of the New Mexico First State Bank, Silver City, New Mexico Territory, U.S.A. That's where he would find Reyas—Silver City—smoking cigars and drinking good liquor in the company of respectful society. It would be easy enough to find him. Slocum folded the paper and put it in his shirt pocket.

"What can we do?" the older man called Hugo asked. Powdered in mine dust like the rest of the men, they and their women sat upon the ground before the mine office.

"Reyas had a legal claim on this mine or he'd never have ran away."

"How, señor, do we get a claim?"

"Hire a lawyer. He can find how to claim it."

"What will that cost?"

"Perhaps hundreds."

The nods went slow through the crowd, then sombreros began to be passed and the clink of their newfound riches soon became their donation.

"Can we sell the silver?"

"You can ship ore like Reyas did. There is no duty on sending ore to the mills at Silver City and do as he did."

"But we would have to send guards?"

"Best. Word will be out those burro train loads are not worthless."

"How will we decide who should be boss?"

"Wait two days, so the dust is settled and then hold an election. A mine boss should be the head man, and his assistant should be able to do his job. You need to pick a leader, not the best friend, but the best boss. Also someone who can count needs to keep the books, be the treasurer."

"Will you stay here and help us, señor?"

He closed his eyes at their request. Maybe he should tell them he stayed nowhere. His sugar-foot ways were necessary for his survival. Even here in the vastness of the Madras, someone would come with a blurred black-and-white sketch of him to collect the bounty.

"For a short while. Some men with horses best go with me to get those prisoners at the cantina and Durango, who is at Magdellania's. Then we can talk of my staying."

Several men nodded and told him they would be ready to ride shortly. He agreed and made small talk until a small boy came riding up on a burro.

"Much *dinero*," he shouted and waved his fistfuls.

"Wait!" Slocum stopped them. "Send a handful to go pick it up. You will need this money to buy stores and other things. Put it all in one fund and we will go from there."

Several were appointed and left to find the scattered currency on the mountain. Slocum checked his own cinch, waiting on the others. He was anxious to see Magdellania. Reminding himself of her promise to share her bed with him, he could hardly wait to get things settled enough to have some time for themselves.

"We are ready to ride and get them," Cruz said and tossed his head to the four other men on horseback.

Slocum swung aboard and checked the horse long enough to settle in the saddle, then they tore out for the village in a hard run. When he swung in Magdellania's yard he expected to see some different horses at the rack. Where was Durango's horse? Niggled by the fact there were none others, but the one she rode down there, he drew his Colt and burst in the front door.

"Magdellania! Magdellania!" No answer. The first thing he spotted were the ropes on the floor that no doubt once had tied the outlaw. His heart sunk and he rushed outside.

"He's gone and so is she."

"Bad news, señor. That Durango is a cruel murderer of women. How long has he been gone?"

Slocum shook his head. He searched in the dust for tracks, joined by the others.

"What should we do now, señor?" Cruz asked.

"Get the prisoners from the cantina if he has not freed them and then I plan to ride after him."

"But the mine, señor? We are uneducated and know nothing about how to operate it."

"Do as I say. Hire a good lawyer to fight for your claim to it. Hire a clerk as Reyas did to do the book work. Send someone to find a smelter who will work your ore and everyone go back to work."

"So many things—" Cruz shook his head. "You think we can do it?"

"Yes, but let no man take it from you."

"I savvy that. What will you do?"

"I will find Durango and her and then return."

"One of us should go with you?"

Slocum shook his head. "All of your men are leaders. The

village and mine will need them. There will be word of this that will get out and like buzzards they will come here to take it over."

"I savvy that, *mi* amigo. But to ride after such a *bastardo* as Durango alone—I worry for you."

"No need," he said and shook each man's hand. Then he ran inside, took a blanket for a bedroll and came out. The men turned their horses and headed for the cantina while he tied it on behind his saddle. He mounted and turned the bay horse west. A tough, small mountain horse, he should carry him a long way. His thoughts about plans were stopped by the sounds of gunfire. He booted the pony and when he could finally see the cantina in the distance, he could make out Cruz standing over a body with a smoking gun. The others too. Justice had been served; Reyas's henchmen had been delivered to hell.

The thing that niggled him more was the fact the real villain, Reyas, had escaped. But Silver City was not hard to find and Reyas's banker was there. He'd find Mr. Cartwright and settle with the outlaw someday, but for the present he needed to catch up with Durango and to find Magdellania unharmed. Anxious to be on his way, he sent the horse off down the south trail.

The horse the outlaw led had a narrow shoe that made an obvious track on the trail. He used that for reference and followed the stream westward. Durango left in much haste, so he did not expect to overtake him for some time. But the grueling pace of galloping on and on would soon wind down his horses, and then Slocum felt certain he would catch up with them.

The sun bore down on him at the lower altitude; the temperature soared. By late afternoon, he saw dust on the horizon. Was it the Ruralists? Perhaps Debrewski had seen the man? He reined up and let the horse rest while he discovered the source of the dirt in the sky.

The red flag that came into sight told him enough. He sent the bay for the column. In the lead, the officer held up his hand for a halt.

Slocum dropped the reins on the bay's neck and took off his hat to wipe his sweaty face on his sleeve.

"Captain?" Slocum nodded in approval at the young messenger who rode with them.

"Ah, my gringo amigo, Slocum, are we too late?" Captain Debrewski asked.

"Good day, sir. The people revolted, Reyas has fled and one of his henchmen has kidnapped a woman and ridden this way." He indicated southerly.

"And his name?"

"All I know is Durango."

The stiff-backed officer turned to his noncom. "Durango?"

"Yes, he is wanted, Captain, for murder and rape and other crimes," his sergeant said.

"Where did he go?" Debrewski asked Slocum.

"He came this way. Obviously he went off the trail when he saw your dust. When they learned you were coming, they all fled."

Debrewski nodded and looked around the flat country that surrounded them. "He no doubt has avoided us. My amigo, how have you been?"

"Good, but I must take up his tracks."

"I will loan you my best trackers. Santos and Miquel, come up here," he shouted.

Two men in khaki uniforms rode up to join them. They carried carbines on their shoulders and ammunition belts across their chests.

"Ride with my amigo, Slocum, and find this Durango. Bring me his head."

They saluted with a "*Si*, Captain."

"Tell them where you saw his tracks last."

"Back there. The horse he leads has a narrow shoe."

The two nodded, saluted and galloped off to the east toward the mountains.

"I will check on the people at the mine this boy spoke about and assure them they only need to send word and I will be there."

"Good. Captain, they plan to run the mine themselves. I

gave them ideas how. Your support would ensure they are not run off." Slocum turned to ride after the two scouts. *"Gracias,"* he said and then he left.

He caught up with the two Ruralists an hour later. They had found the track where Durango headed southward. Here the desert bristled with cholla and spiny cousins, and the strong smell of creosote hung like a curtain on the hot winds in their faces.

"This *hombre* is bad," the shorter one, Miquel, said.

Slocum agreed.

"He raped a young girl in a village, then used his knife on her." Miquel shook his head. "He's crazy."

"Why we must catch him. He has a good woman with him," Slocum said as they stood in the saddle and trotted their horses. Bitter dust boiled up in their faces, clogging their eyes and noses.

"There will be water at the village of Aqua ahead," Santos said. "He may stop there."

"Be fine with me," Slocum said.

They arrived at the small village spread about under some lacy mesquite shade. The desert trees were the only things not dirt brown like the hovels the people lived in. Even the burros looked near starved. No dogs barked—they no doubt had been eaten and the few residents looked drawn with their eyes in deep sockets. Somewhere in their distance, a baby cried.

"We look for a man and a woman," Santos said to the woman who came out to the well.

"Si," she said and swept her arm toward the south. "He left, maybe a while ago."

"Was the woman all right?" Slocum asked.

"She looked worried. But she was unharmed," the woman said, using her hand to shade her eyes so she could see him against the last red glow of sundown.

He nodded he heard her.

"I could trade you for some food," she said and tried to smile.

Busy dipping a bucket from the well to water the animals,

Santos nodded. To her he said, "We have no time and little food ourselves."

She dropped her chin. "I have no food and plenty of time."

The horses crowded the trough when he dumped each pail of water into the trough. Slocum dismounted, rummaged in his saddlebags and found some jerky wrapped in paper.

"It is dry," he said, handing it to her.

"You want me?" she asked with a head toss toward the doorway behind her.

"Not now," he said softly.

"I can't pay you."

He put his arm around her and hugged her. She felt so thin, it made him sick. "You don't owe me anything."

"May God bless you, señor."

"Slocum."

She nodded and repeated his name. "Slo-cum."

"Your name?"

"I'm Elania."

"Go with God, Elania."

Tears in the corners of her eyes, she grasped the small package of jerky to her dress. "No, he should ride with you, señor."

She nodded and, unable to control her sorrow, she ran back inside. He watched her disappear and then turned his attention to Santos and Miquel's efforts to pull enough water up for the still thirsty horses.

"It has not rained here in a long time," Miquel said as other villagers young and old stared at them from their doorways and the corners of buildings.

Slocum nodded he understood and sighed, sipping water from a yellow gourd that Santos handed him. Taking slow sips, he felt the coolness slip down his throat and cut the trail of dust that coated the route downward.

"Where shall we camp?" Miquel asked.

"Ride south until it is too dark to see," Slocum said and both men quickly agreed, obviously not anxious to stay in Aqua under the dire circumstances.

Canteens refilled, horses watered, they tightened their

cinches and left the silent village. Slocum turned back as the last bloodred of the sundown fired the huts in crimson. How long could they hold out? No rain. No clouds. No hope, he decided and set the bay after the others.

The pony acted reprieved by the water, but Slocum knew without grain or forage, their animals would soon tire and stumble on their feet. In the last of twilight, they made camp in a draw, found some sticks for their fire and hobbled the ponies to let them snatch the powder-dry weeds for themselves.

Over the small campfire, they boiled their cups of *pulcia* and leisurely ate their supper.

"Think," Santos said, looking in his cup for the next spoonful. "You could have spent the night with her for two cents' worth of jerky."

"We would have waited for you," Miquel said with a big grin.

"How far ahead is Durango?" Slocum asked, more interested in the distance separating them from the outlaw and Magdellania than the thin girl's body.

"Half a day, maybe less," Miquel said.

Slocum nodded in approval. "Tomorrow we can celebrate, *mi* amigos, when we have his head in a sack."

Both men nodded at him and grew silent. Slocum heard nothing in the night but the snort of their weary horses searching for anything to eat. Too dry in this land for the wily coyotes or even the fiddles of the cicadas. The eerie deep silence had an unsettling effect on him as he finished his last spoonful and rolled a cigarette. Hard too, to consider the conditions of life for Elania and her poor fellow villagers. He closed his eyes to shut out the day. But in his heart, he knew there would be more like them.

11

Durango sneered at the small rancher who came out from under the shade of the ramada holding his worn straw sombrero before him.

"What may I do for you, señor?" the man asked.

"I want to buy fresh horses."

"Oh, señor, I have only some ponies."

"Get them," Durango said, dismounting and undoing his cinch. "I'll pay you and give you these two in trade."

"But, señor—"

"Go get the horses and they better be good," he said, waving latigo leathers as he uncinched the saddle. "Get down and unsaddle," he said to Magdellania, who still sat on the head-down roan.

Numbly she obeyed, her fingers fumbling at the wet leather until, filled with impatience, he stepped in between her and the horse.

"You aren't fast enough."

"I was trying. I've had no sleep—"

"Sleep! You can sleep in hell." He anxiously looked to the east where the first shafts of the sun crested the line of purple mountains. From the corner of his eye he could see a young woman with a baby in a bundle. He read the worry in her eyes—she knew what he stood for; she knew at another time, he would plow his dick into her until she fainted. This one who lived so far away from civilization—even she knew the awesome power he had over women.

Something he would teach the bitch Magdellania before he was through with her. He jerked the undone saddle off the roan's back. In surrender the horse's knees buckled and he lay down like a cow—a sign that he was through. The sounds coming from the animal's throat also had warned Durango the animal would not last long. A moaning noise of death only spent horses made that he knew well.

The two horses the rancher led up looked bony. Their hips stuck out and their bodies resembled greyhounds. Still, he knew these two could get them to Arroyo Grande. There he would buy, steal or whatever some better ones. He tossed his saddle on the narrow-necked gray, cinching it up, and he shouted for her to put hers on the dun.

"These are my best ones," the man said softly.

"I see that," Durango said, ignoring him and going to the other horse. He ripped the saddle from her hands and tossed it on the other gelding. Then he reached underneath and grabbed the girth. In minutes, he had the saddle screwed down and motioned for her to mount.

The dun leaned over under her weight when she mounted him. Still, he tongued the bit and that satisfied Durango that these two had more life than the bay crusted in dried salt.

"What do I owe you?" Durango said, adjusting his stirrup to mount up.

"Señor, your horses will die they are so tired," the man said, shaking his head in disapproval.

"I say it is a good trade, huh, amigo?"

The man shook his head, not looking up.

"Not so good then?"

A pain-filled look on his face, the short rancher nodded as he squinted against the sun's new flare. "Those are my best horses."

"Mine too," Durango said, looking at their back trail for any sign of pursuit.

"But, señor—"

Durango whipped out his pistol and shot the man in the chest. "I'll give you five centavos' worth of lead for them." The gray moved around under him, excited by the blast.

The man sunk to the ground. His fingers pressed to his chest, blood rushing out between them. From the ramada, the young woman came screaming—crying out his name.

"Get out of here!" Durango shouted at Magdellania. He rode in close and whipped the dun on the butt with his reins. They fled through the head-high mesquite and soon were headed south again.

"Why did you kill him?" Magdellania demanded.

"Because he complained!"

She asked no more of him as they raced across the empty desert. Durango knew Grande Arroyo was still a good day's ride ahead of them. There he would wash down the dust in his parched throat with some tequila, find a bed and split in half that straight-backed bitch's crotch. The notion amused him; he laughed aloud, rode in close to her, and again he slashed her dun with his reins. He would show her.

Darkness swallowed the day. The hoof drop of their spent horses on the hard-packed street of Grande Arroyo sounded loud. Light from inside the houses and stores made a patchwork of yellow on the narrow street between the two rows of buildings. Drunken men staggered from the cantinas into the street and raised their bottles to salute them. Somewhere a trumpet played and the sounds of a fiddle cut the night's hot air radiating off the adobe buildings like a reflective furnace.

"Fandango" escaped his lips.

One unsteady drunk came out of a cantina, raised his bottle and shouted, "Fiesta time!"

Durango reined his horse in close, swiped the bottle from the man's hand and turned it up.

"Viva Mexico!" he shouted and leaned back to avoid the

drunk's attempt to recover it. At last, he shook his right leg out of the stirrup and planted his sole in the man's chest, sending him reeling backward.

"My bottle—" the man cried, seated on his butt in the dust.

"Finders keepers," Durango said, amused, and took another drink from the bottle. A few more swigs might cut the desert's dust. "Losers weepers," he said to himself as they rode on.

He turned in the saddle to glare at her. She would be the one to cry tonight all right. Soon too. Then he saw the Chinese lanterns and the couples dancing in the square.

"Ah, señora," he said leaning back in the saddle to look at her. "We got here just in time to enjoy ourselves. Hey, fiesta!"

She never answered.

"You say a word to these people and I will kill all of them," he said in a stage whisper. He reined up the gray and looked at her hard.

Her eyes glared with hatred, but she gave him a sharp nod that she understood.

"Good," he said. "Let's stable these horses. I think your amigo Slocum never found our trail." Then he laughed aloud to taunt her. They were a long ways from that bastard.

Perhaps he should circle back and find Reyas in New Mexico. No, first he would give him time to think he was safe—he laughed some more. Wouldn't that be the day, when he faced that *bastardo* and demanded his pay and interest.

Tonight, he had the best-looking woman in the camp to show off. Magdellania. First, he would drink and dance and eat and forget the damn hot ride to this hellhole in the rectum of the world—Grande Arroyo.

"May I care for your horse, *Patrón*?" a young boy asked, running barefoot alongside him.

"Grain, water and good hay?"

"*Si,* señor."

Durango swung down and when the boy took the reins, his hand shot out and grasped the boy's privates in his fist. He leaned over to speak in the squirming one's ear.

"If these horses are not ready to ride in the morning I will cut them off below your belly and you can squat to pee, hear me?"

"I will! I will, señor." The desperate boy tried to escape his hold. He cried out as Durango increased his grip.

"Remember what I say."

"I promise, señor, please . . ."

Durango let go and the boy doubled over in pain, holding himself. He jerked him up by his ear. "You mess up, I promise you will squat to piss like a *puta*."

"No. No," the boy moaned.

"Get her horse too," he said and the boy staggered over to obey him.

"Come," he said to her, impatience ringing in his tone. "What is your name?"

"Tomas," the boy said with difficulty, holding himself with one hand.

"You heard me. What are you standing there for? Go and feed and water them."

The boy nodded and jerked the horses after him into the darkness.

A sly smile in the corner of his mouth, he held out his arm for her to take.

"Someone will cut yours out and feed them to you someday," she said in low whisper.

"Ah and you would enjoy seeing that?"

"Definitely."

"You will die of old age before that happens, girl," he said and drew her along to the lighted area where the couples danced.

He whirled her around on the dance floor. Her firm breasts crushed against his chest. He envisioned what they looked like. His hips ached to probe her. Heady from the tequila, he soon decided it was time to find a place for her first lesson. He guided her into the shadows. His whiskered mouth kissed her neck and his hand fondled her breast underneath the thin material of her blouse.

"You need to be drunk," he said, raising back and staring

at her when she did not respond to his actions. This cold bitch needed some mescal in her blood. She'd get mellow then—he'd never seen such a chilly woman. Of course, he had not had much experience with such a highbrow one before. Most of his conquests were stupid peons, *putas* or Indian wenches from the mountains, like the slut at the mines when he choked her—she went out of this world in the arms of passion.

"Come," he said, jerking her by the arm. "I'm getting you drunk."

"No."

He slapped her hard across the face. The music stopped and he glared around. "Sing, she's my wife. I'll slap her when she needs it."

The music quickly restarted and several men nodded in approval. They fed his ego and he smiled. Those *hombres* knew how to handle a bitch. At the bar, he ordered two glasses of mescal. The bartender set them up and stood ready for Durango to pay him. But Durango never looked at the man, motioning for her to take one.

She refused.

"Drink it or wish you had," he said through his teeth.

She relented, stepped up and downed the glass. The liquor choked her and she coughed, clutched her throat, bent over the bar. Pale-faced, she swallowed and at last stood.

"Now that one," he pointed at glass, then crossed his arms waiting for her to obey.

She picked up the glass, chewed on her lower lip, then with resolve put the rim to her lip and managed to down half the contents. Out of breath, she set the glass down and fought to regain her breathing.

"The rest."

She nodded she heard him and tried to drink again. This time in several gulps she downed it. He moved in and hugged her shoulders. "Now you will not resist me," he said privately in her ear.

He paid the man and then headed her for the street. Already she reeled on her feet. He knew he must hurry. Too much liquor was as bad as not enough. A room in the hotel and he would have her body all to himself.

"What—now?" she slurred and he caught her before she fell forward and he dragged her backward into the shadow.

Something down the street had caught his eye. Three riders—two by their hats looked like Ruralists, the third a civilian, not Mexican either by his moves. Durango's calloused palm clamped over her mouth, and he dragged her back deeper into the space between the buildings.

What would he do next? The huge, pulsating erection in his pants hurt him. The excruciating stone ache in his left testicle nauseated him and the damn law with Slocum had shown up.

12

Reyas rode a stout mule. His horse gave out and the solution was to buy the large mule. The man who sold it to him said it was one that the Comanches bred. The sun brand on his shoulder was a sure sign he came from them. Reyas didn't care about his mount's source; he thought the jackass was a spook. The black animal spent most of the time peddling sideways as well as acting up from the small crossroads in Mexico where they bought him until they reached the Southern Pacific tracks at Demming.

There a train locomotive hooted its horn at a crossing and the ass went wild, bucking down the street, issuing great farts and wringing his tail with each one. When Reyas came back on foot leading the animal and pulling down on the crotch of his pants, he was ready to sell the mule and buy a horse. Surely, in a town this large he could find a suitable horse.

"Oh, *patrón*." Alphanso came hurrying to meet him on his short-backed brown horse.

Only worse, that was the reason why Reyas did not make the boy ride the mule instead of him. That sorry horse was even harder riding than the long-eared SOB he led up the street. Reyas spun around looking for a livery sign. A cowboy came down the road, riding a dish-faced mare. Out of breath and patience Reyas hailed him down.

"How would you trade that fine mare for my mule, mister?"

The cowboy used his thumb to raise the felt hat and leaned back in the saddle to examine the jackass.

"Why, mister, I guess I'd trade for fifty bucks," he drawled.

"That's saddle and all?" Reyas asked, not anxious to go through all the effort to have to switch his to the mare.

"I reckon," the cowboy said and dismounted.

Reyas dug in his pocket and paid the man in gold coins. "She ain't worth that much, but I need something to ride. Good luck with that gawdamn mule."

"Obliged," the cowboy said, busy counting his fortune while Reyas mounted the mare and turned her around.

"Come on, Alphanso, we need to find a hotel," he said. Unable not to watch, he stayed to see the cowboy leap in the saddle and head out in a hard trot straight down the street without a single problem, except for the mule's farting and wringing his tail. No bucking or running away whatsoever— he shook his head in disgust.

Reyas turned to see the boy's horse arching his neck and pawing the ground.

"What's the matter with him?" he demanded.

"This horse of mine is proud cut."

"Proud cut?"

"Yes, and that new mare of yours is horsing."

"Oh, mother of God! What next? You keep that damn horse of yours away from her then." He waved at the boy to get back.

"*Si, Patrón,* I will ride a block behind you."

"Good. We will put them in the livery stable up the street. I saw one."

"*Si, Patrón.*"

Another stallion screamed and Reyas jerked around. Damn, what else would go wrong? He'd breed this pretty mare to one of his fine stallions at Silver City if he lived that long. He booted her for the stables before one of the studs in the street tried to mount her with him on board.

At last, after a dinner of tough beef and rock-hard boiled potatoes, they went to the hotel and found a room. Reyas looked out the window at the mountains in the distance. Silver City awaited him, with his riches in the bank vault and still more loads to be smelted. Money enough to do what he wanted. He raised his arms over his head and stretched. It would be nice to be a rich American; perhaps he could marry some rich American girl and have children. Money made you respectable, he knew that as he watched the supply train loaded with new rails chug out for the West and the project to join the line coming from California.

In the morning, they ate breakfast among the railroad workers that smelled of grease and oil. They spoke about their locomotives and the boiler problems with the hard water they'd encountered in the West. Already through eating, Reyas picked his teeth with a toothpick, waiting for the boy to finish his meal.

He could hardly look over at the demented lad and not recall seeing him mounted on the other one, jacking him away. He shuddered at the notion. The sooner he got rid of him, the better—first he had to know more about his banking situation since Alphanso set it all up.

Perhaps the mare wouldn't be in heat—or it would be over. He was anxious to get there and find a residence—even a ranch of his own. Would that boy not hurry up—he ate so slow he wanted to clout him.

In thirty minutes, they were trotting north through the desert for Silver City. The trip would require all day, even at a trot, but he wanted to be there. Perhaps if they rode that proud-cut bastard long enough, it would take the hard pecker out of him too. Besides, the mare was fresh and full of vim. His eyes on the far off mountains, they rode on.

They found a small store near midday, watered their animals at the tank under a windmill and then went inside. Reyas thought the crowd at the table playing cards looked tough, but he ignored them. Still he knew the Colt on his hip and the other in his waistband were loaded if they turned into *banditos*.

"Some jerky?" he asked the man, not wanting any long-gone-sour fresh meat.

"Si."

"Give us each a fistful," he said and dug in his pockets for the money.

"Ha," someone said in a loud voice. In the corner of his eye, Reyas saw him stand over the table.

He motioned for the boy to get his fistful of the brown twisted meat. Were they about to be challenged? Alphanso took it from the man—Reyas thinking all the while he hoped that Alphanso held them in a different hand than he used on that boy.

"Mister! We get a tariff for anyone using that road out there." He was huge hulk of a man with a long beard and tobacco stains around his wide mouth that looked red when he opened it to speak.

"Ah!" Reyas said. "Like a ferryboat, huh?"

"Yeah," he said and the other two at the table chuckled.

" 'Cept I charge Mexicans more."

"Oh."

"You want to know why?"

"Certainly."

" 'Cause they're greasers, that's why!" He laughed raucously at him. Then his face turned to shock when the Colt in Reyas's hand spewed orange flames. Cut down by one of Reyas's bullets, the big man sunk to the floor.

"Oh, gawd, I'm shot, boys. Help me? Please help me."

"How much we owe you?" Reyas asked in the cloud of blue smoke that made everyone in the place cough.

"Nothing, señor. Nothing, señor," the man said, about to cry.

Reyas thanked him, backing for the door, hoping Alphanso had gone for their horses. He heard some cussing and some pounding. Where was that damn boy? He held the pistol out to show them he'd use it. The big man was on his back moaning and cussing Mexicans. He wanted to go over and finish him off for that—where was Alphanso?

"Señor!"

He backed out the door and looked at his clerk and the two horses.

"I had to disengage them," Alphanso said and shook his head.

Reyas put a bullet in the ceiling of the store, knowing the dust and gun smoke would distract them. He ran for his mount and flew into the saddle. On his mare at last, they raced over the loose, sandy road for Silver City.

"Who were those guys?" Alphanso asked.

"Damned if I know. All I know, I'm not paying no fee to ride this road."

"Me either," Alphanso said and looked back with a fear-filled expression.

"Nothing coming back there?"

"No, I see no one."

"Good." Perhaps they learned a lesson not to mess with him. He felt better riding the mare than at any time since they left the mine at Vaca. Perhaps in Silver City, he would find some *puta* to entertain him for the night. Perhaps get one for Alphanso too and maybe she could teach him how to do it right. No, once a queer, you would always be one. Too late for him—he hurried his mare northward.

Late in the evening, bone tired from the long ride, they left their horses at a livery. They found a cafe and ate some hot food cooked by a plump Mexican woman named Maria with *grande* boobs. One thing led to another and Reyas became so infatuated with her that he sent the boy off to find a hotel room by himself. With two bottles of red wine, he and Maria went to her place a block away.

"Ah, I have needed a real man for some time," she said and gave him an elbow in the gut.

"You needed a real one, huh?"

"I don't mean some boy with a weeny like my finger," she said and opened the door. Then she laughed raucously with her head thrown back. "You got a bigger one than that, Rey?"

"Lots bigger than that," he said, looking up and down the dark street. Nothing out of place, so he followed her inside. She lit a candle lamp on the table, then took him in a great hug and began to kiss him. With a wine bottle in both hands, he was helpless but enjoyed her attention. Soon her hand ran over the crotch of his pants and she shouted, *"Grande! Muy grande!"*

Then it was set the wine down, tear off their clothes and get naked.

Her laughter would wake the dead—he didn't care, toeing off his boots and shucking his pants. She tore the cork out of one wine bottle with her teeth and spit it away.

"To great lovemaking," she toasted to the ceiling and turned it up. Dark liquid in the dim light ran from the sides of her mouth. She shoved the bottle into his bare chest for him to drink. He turned it up in time to about choke when her hands grasped his scrotum and began to fondle his testicles in her hand.

In a minute, she was in the bed and he took another deep draught for strength. "Ah, Maria!" he shouted and the ropes groaned under the bed.

With his half-hard dick in his hand, he waded forward between her thick outstretched legs and poked it into her. She gave the cry of a woman in pleasure and he went to work on her. Kneading her great breasts, he pumped his hips to go deeper and deeper until he reached the great belly, giving her all he had.

"Oh! Oh!" she cried. "So *grande!* So *grande!*"

He worked harder and harder. His breath grew shorter, the muscles in his rectum tightened and then he felt an explosion rising in his balls. He pushed as hard as he could against her—he gave her the final salvo in a pain-filled blast out the overexpanded head of his dick.

A short cry caught in her throat, she fainted limp in a pile and his head swam. Suddenly he felt the entire ride from Mexico, the damn stiff mule that bucked him off, all the miles and the muscles in his back ached in spasms. There he knelt with his fading hard-on still in her, between her huge

sausage-like legs and up against the mountainous belly, looking at some melon-size breasts that suddenly lost all their
appeal. Ugh.

He awoke the next morning to a rooster crowing.

"What do you do?" she asked.

He looked up and saw she was wearing a thin cotton gown.
Too much woman for him. What did she ask?

"I don't care what you do. I have a business. I make good
money. You can stay here—with me. I will feed you well
and we can make love, no?"

"No, sorry." He sat up and combed his hair back with his
fingers.

"You are married. Never mind, you can come here anyway."

He held his hands up to silence her. "I am a businessman.
I came here from Mexico to do business with Cartwright at
the bank. So I must go."

She shook her head in disbelief and hooded her left eye
to frown at him. "You're a businessman? You dress like a
vaquero? You screw like a stallion, and you don't look like
no businessman to me."

"Disguise. Who do the *banditos* rob? People with money
who dress fancy and ride fine horses?"

"*Si,* but—" She folded her thick arms over her great trea-
sures and shook her head. "No, I am not convinced who you
are. But when you need some again, come and see me." She
turned and the gown flowed around her large form.

"What do you want in this world?" he asked, picking up
his pants and shaking them in case a scorpion had crawled
inside them during the night. Then, on his feet, he began to
pull them on.

"A great diamond to wear around my neck," she said,
looking out the back door into the yard.

"My clerk, Alphanso, will bring you one before the sun
sets."

She glanced back over her shoulder at him as he tucked
in his shirt. "Why?"

"You were generous. Why can't I be?"

"What do you want?"

"Nothing."

"Ha, when you are horny again, come back," she said and turned away.

He put on his holster. "I will. Do you know someone good with figures and books?"

"My cousin has a son been to Sante Fe, he studied there."

"What does he do?"

"Makes adobe bricks."

"Why?"

"Who needs a Mexican to count his money, huh?" She rolled a cigarette from corn husks and he could smell the sharp smoke of her tobacco.

"I do. I need to have two clerks. What is his name?"

"Ramon."

"Good, he can learn from Alphanso. Tell him to come find me today."

"Where will you be?"

"Which hotel is the best?"

"The Royal."

"I will be there. Tell him to ask for Señor Estevan Reyas from Vaca, Sonora."

"What do they call you?"

"Estevan Reyas."

She nodded, but still eyed him with a look of doubt. "Maybe you are some lying vaquero with a big dick between your legs. I will see."

He put on his sombrero and went off to find his clerk. Soon he would have a new one; he never asked her if this boy liked girls. What would a diamond cost? He had never bought one before—before he had the workers' wives and daughters, and he only gave them blankets or some more credit at the store. That big woman might be good to know— he would bet she knew everything that happened in Silver City. He would send her a diamond.

Where was Alphanso? His head hurt and he needed a drink. The boy would show up, so he pushed his way into a cantina. Whiskey would help.

13

Slocum and the two Ruralists made their way toward the music. Their horses were already in the stable. The next thing to do was to look for Durango. Filled with concern for Magdellania's safety in the hands of the bloody killer, Slocum's boot heels hit the gritty ground as he hurried toward the Chinese lanterns.

"Ah, señor," a slightly drunk señorita greeted him and swung on his arm. "What brings you to Arroyo?"

"A man with red hair. Tough looking."

"Ah, you are too late. He left an hour ago."

"She said he was here and left an hour ago," he said to the others.

"Damn, I need some food and wine." Miquel shook his head. "How far can he go?"

"Did he get fresh horses?" Slocum asked her.

"I guess so. He and his wife left here."

"Was she all right?"

"I guess so. He got her drunk."

Wife? He frowned at her words. "Why did he make her drink?"

"Cause, she was acting so stiff. No fun. You know. Come,

all of you. Ruralists, we have food and wine." She forced Slocum toward the table and other women brought some of the cooked steer on a platter.

"We have to eat them or they will die without rain, no?" the girl asked, pressing her rock-hard tit into Slocum's arm as she straddled the bench beside him.

"How drunk was she?"

"Oh, a few drinks. She will enjoy her night. Will you?"

"It depends," he said, realizing how hungry he had grown with only the *pulcia* to feed him for days. The mesquite-roasted meat was tough and stringy, but the flavor was mouthwatering. He set in to eat his full share and asked the woman about all she had seen and knew about the red-headed stranger while he fed himself. She helped him, pouring his wine and keeping his glass full.

He was busy eating his fill. But Magdellania was more on his mind than the attractive, dark-eyed woman who sat beside him. How far had he gone with her? They needed to capture him and do it quickly. How much had Durango forced her to drink?

In the dark stables, Durango had trouble holding her up and moving close to the walls. He could hear their weary horses snorting and blowing. Where were his? Then in a shaft of starlight he saw the gray's head—still saddled. He let the moaning Magdellania slip to the ground. In a flash he was beside the horses. Still saddled, the manger before them was empty. Without feed, they would be unable to stand another night's ride. He gritted his teeth, looking to be certain that no one was coming in the stable's alleyway from the street. Those Ruralists and the gringo would soon know he had been here.

He found two sound horses and led them back. In a flash, he exchanged saddles, stopping twice for fear he had been discovered, then when the drunken person went by the front entrance, he resumed his work. Both saddled, he went to where she lay.

Passed out. He would have to tie her belly-down over the

saddle. That required more time. At last, with her limp body slung over the saddle, he prepared to leave. He was still angry about the boy's poor job of caring for the two horses— he fought back the urge to kill him. Where was that boy anyway?

Durango searched around and soon found a room. On the door facing, he scratched a match and spotted the "liar" lying in the corner on some sacks. His lips pursed, he blew out the light. Then he turned on his heels and went to the front of the stable where the tinder-crisp fodder was stacked. He struck a match and soon the flames began to lick at the stems.

Then he walked back to the room, knife in hand. He dragged the half-asleep boy into the alleyway and ripped off his shorts with the slash of his blade. Next he grasped the boy's manhood in his fist.

"My God!" the boy screamed at the top of his lungs when the blade flashed again, this time severing off his sack and all.

"Next time you will listen." Durango dropped the bloody handful in the dirt and stood back.

Shakily on his feet, the boy held himself, staggering around and yowling in pain. Then in a broken gait, he rushed through the stables, screaming at the top of his lungs. Durango watched him stagger through the growing wall of fire into the street.

He mounted his new horse, taking the lead of the other, and left out the back way. The fire had begun to crackle. But even as he went over the last ridge, the boy's incessant screams continued until the night swallowed them.

She awoke puking. He stopped with the sour vapors up his nose and stepped off the horse, letting her down.

"Oh," she groaned. Swaying around, she finally put her hands on her knees to brace herself and had the dry heaves. "Damn you, Durango!"

"That's what that boy said."

"What boy?"

"The one who didn't do what I told him, so I castrated him."

"You what?" She wiped her hand on the back of her mouth, looking in disbelief at him.

"I cut him. He didn't listen."

"You're despicable. Utterly despicable."

"You don't want the same kind of treatment, get over here."

She blinked in disbelief at him, but she stood her ground. The muscles in his jaw tightened, and he wanted to go over and slap her around until she begged him to stop. "Get on that horse. We've got miles to ride. Them damn Ruralists like to have caught us back there."

When he looked back, he saw nothing on the star-lighted horizon and turned back to her. She had obeyed him and gotten on the other horse. Good—when they got a safe enough distance, he'd show her a thing or two.

Flames billowed out of the stables; the screaming boy was dragged away from harm's way and a doctor sent for. Slocum rushed around behind the building and broke through the thinner flames and with his knife began slashing leads and waving his arms at the panicked horses.

"I'll lead some out," Santos shouted and took two by the rope and headed for the back door. Animals reared and plunged in excitement. One knocked Slocum aside as he reached to slash the rope free. The heat of the fire scorched his face as he cut loose even more. Bumped and kicked at, he ignored his own safety and worked to free more even if turned loose they wouldn't chance the escaping due to the flames on the floor before the back door.

Other men joined him and began to beat the flames out with blankets and pads. Others led the excited horses out. Some overwrought horses jerked free and rushed back into the inferno engulfing the front half of the stables. With Slocum's eyes stinging, there was no more he could do, and he latched onto the halter of a wide-eyed horse. It ran backward until someone hit it in the butt with his blanket, then it ran over him, leaping across the smoking litter and dragging him halfway down the alley before he could stop it.

"All we can do!" someone shouted and they backed up.

Someone mercifully shot a horse with his mane and hair on fire trapped in the building. Still, the sounds of the other trapped animals inside the stables proved disconcerting. Slocum was bent over, coughing from his heat- and smoke-seared lungs.

"Señor." The woman from the dance handed him a glass of liquid. Her hand was on his shoulder to steady him; the mescal cut a trail down his throat. He nodded in approval at her. Someone else handed her a wet rag and she began to wipe off his face.

"You are too much of an *hombre*. You could have died in there," she said in disapproval.

"The boy?"

"He died, lost too much blood. Only an animal would do such a thing."

"Yes," he said and looked off into the darkness.

"Plenty crazy."

His breath returning, he noticed the two Ruralists bringing their horses up.

"They are fine," Santos said. "Only a few hairs singed, but we watered them and they are ready."

"So am I," Slocum said. He grabbed the woman in his arms, kissed her long and hard on the mouth. Tasted the honey on her hot tongue before he quit. Then when he let her go, looked deep into her eyes. "Such a shame, but I must stop him."

"Cut his *huevos* out for me!" she shouted and slapped him on the shoulder.

He nodded he had heard her and mounted his horse. The familiar smell of burned leather and hair like at branding time filled his nose. The roof collapsed on the stables and an outrush of smoke engulfed them in the alley.

"*Vaya con Dios!*" she shouted as the three rode out to the street.

May God be with you too. His eyes still smarted from the smoke, so he followed their lead. Durango deserved all that he would receive from them. Ruralists were not famous for bringing in prisoners; the legal system in Sonora was so corrupt, they solved it and brought few back alive. It saved feeding them and also the cost of a trial, plus it sent a clear message to the banditry. You mess with the law in the northern states of Mexico, expect the sentence for the crime to be administered by the muzzle of a carbine or a pistol shot behind the left ear.

The three rode through the night. Slocum could look back and see the glow of the fire in the sky for several hours as they rode south. Those people would be lucky if it didn't set more of the town ablaze than that. Obviously they had no quantity of water to put it out with either.

"Perhaps he will ride to Doña next," Santos offered, leading his horse through the greasewood and looking for tracks.

"We need to hurry before he kills some more innocent people," Slocum said, still feeling the searing inside his chest. No time for hurting; they needed to stop Durango before he hurt Magdellania. How had he managed to load her drunk on a horse and still get away? Somewhere he had seriously underestimated this enemy—not only was he brutal beyond comprehension, but there was no end to his butchery.

The sun was coming up behind the Madras and the flannel light filtered into the desert basin. Dark shapes of the jackals of Dona dotted the barren ground. No fires, no lights, no dog barks, but Slocum knew their absence had become the way since the eternal drought held all the desert people in a bench vise–like grip, slowly strangling them to death.

"How should we ride in?" Santos asked, standing in the stirrups and peering at the silent village before them in the distance.

"Circle," Slocum said. "He expects us to ride in and think we never guessed he would be there."

"Maybe he rode on," Miquel said. But neither man took his bait.

"That bastard is down there, if he stole the best horses in the stables," Santos promised his *compadre*. "He is waiting to shoot or knife you too."

Satisfied, Miquel nodded with the outline of his peaked hat against the lighting sky.

"Let me enter the village," Slocum said. "One of you watch the south, the other the north. Don't shoot the woman."

"We won't," both agreed.

"Good, but get him at any price."

"The bastard is dead if he comes out or if we too must go in and get him. I swear on my mother's grave."

"Good enough," Slocum said, tightening his cinch and remounting. He gave them a wave and headed for Dona.

In a dry wash, he dismounted and let the reins drag. The pony was ground broke and stood quietly snorting in the dirt from weariness. With the Colt in his hand, Slocum climbed the bank and surveyed the dark residences. Strange that no one stirred. No woman made a fire. No housewife swept her house and sprinkled water on the floor to settle the dust. No baby cried.

The skin on the back of his neck prickled with electricity. He reached the side of the first hovel, listened—nothing. Had they abandoned the entire village? The drought, the hard times, the bandits that roamed the countryside. He eased his way with the gun ready to the front. Hammer back, he swiftly came around the corner.

A rasping call made him stop; he considered the direction and spotted someone crawling on their belly from a doorway. Was it a trap? He couldn't understand their words, only they were pleading.

With care, he hurried over and after a quick check knelt down and rolled the man over. He'd been shot. Even in the shadowy light, he could see where the dark blood covered the man's ragged shirt.

"Who shot you?"

"A stranger," the man gasped. "I know not his name—I said, there's no *agua* here and he shot me."

"No water?" Slocum asked, holding the man in his lap.

"Went dry—why they all left months ago."

"Why were you here?"

"Came back for some of my things. . . ." The voice grew

weaker and then the man's eyes closed. Same ones only minutes before that had pleaded for his help then half opened in a blankness that told Slocum his heart had stopped. And the pain was gone—forever.

He set the dead man down gently, rose to his feet and went to the edge of the buildings. "Come on in! He's not here, he's gone on!" His voice cut the quiet and soon Santos appeared on his low-headed horse coming toward the abandoned village. Miquel rode in too. Score another death to Durango.

The notion only added to the weight on Slocum's mind. Magdellania. Was she all right? He looked to the south. How far to *agua*?

14

"So grand to finally meet you, Señor Reyas," the broad-shouldered man in the suit said, standing up behind his polished desk to clutch his hand.

"My clerk, Alphanso, told me all about you, señor. The pleasure is mine."

"Speaking of the mine. How is it, señor?"

"Oh, the bandits drove me out."

"Drove you out?"

"Yes, they are so bad in Mexico that I have come to live here in Silver City. I need to buy a ranch—"

"Is there no way the government down there will help you? It was such a rich mine." The man looked shaken by Reyas's losses.

"Ah, don't worry, there is a pack train today at the smelter and two more on the way here, all heavily laden."

"That is such good news," the man said, drying his palms on his pants. "So good to see you finally in person."

"Me too. Alphanso told me so much about how kind you treated him."

"A great customer like you, señor, needs good care. Now,

your horse man and the stallions are at my ranch. They are all cared for well out there."

"Good, but I will need to look for a ranch for myself."

"The horses are fine at my place. Relax, no need to rush out and do anything rash."

"Nothing rash, but I would like a house of my own."

"No problem, you may have the house on Boulder Street."

"Good, how much does it cost?"

"It belongs to my bank. For you, nothing."

"Wonderful, I am ready to move in."

"I'll have my man show you the dwelling. Where is Alphanso?" He searched around for the boy.

"I guess he must have slept in," Reyas said to apologize. "I have not seen him since we parted last night."

"I am sure he is all right. He comes here often and knows the town very well."

"Si. Si." Damn, he must learn to talk less Spanish and more English if he planned to live in this country.

"My man, Baker, will drive you up there? Much luggage?"

"Hardly any, we barely managed to get out with our lives."

"What a shame. And that rich mine is now in the hands of bandits?"

"Bandits," he said solemnly and nodded his dropped head.

"Come, you need some rest," Cartwright said and herded him out of his office. In the lobby, the banker summoned a younger man to drive him to the house on Boulder Street.

"Be certain that Señor Reyas is comfortable," Cartwright said to the young man.

"I will, sir. This way, Señor Reyas." He turned to his boss and said, "I'll see that Mr. Reyas is going to be fine there, sir."

"Very good, Baker. Señor Reyas is an important depositor."

"See you later and then we can talk about buying a ranch," Reyas said, shaking the man's hand again.

"No rush," Cartwright said. "Don't be in any hurry."

"I won't, since you are feeding my stallions and providing me a casa."

Cartwright clapped him on the shoulder. "Don't worry, we can take care of everything."

Reyas felt good going out the door after the smartly dressed young man. Perhaps he needed some clothes like that—Maria thought he was some poor vaquero, not a rich businessman. Oh well, he liked his leather pants and when you're rich who cares what people think. There could be wealthy vaqueros too. He was one.

Where was that Alphanso? He blinked his eyes going out in the bright sun.

"Señor?" A young man with his straw sombrero held before him stood on the boardwalk.

"I am Ramon—my aunt—"

Reyas's fingers on his mouth silenced him. This young banker did not need to know his business. "Good, say no more. Come along, we go to my casa."

I have—"

"Yes." He cut the youth's words off and directed him to the waiting surrey. "Get in back. I will ride with Señor Baker."

"Buzz, sir. They call me Buzz," the young banker said to him.

"Good, Buzz, take me and Ramon to this house."

He sat up straight on the seat beside the young man. His arms were folded over his leather jacket. Maybe he should get a suit, be a businessman in New Mexico. He would think about that later.

The house was set under some juniper trees and had a porch that beckoned to him. A very *norte americano*-style casa, but he liked it. Inside the furniture was sparse, but he shrugged it off. The woman with the big tits would know where to find a cook and a housekeeper. Or this new boy would know—Ramon, yes, Ramon would find him a good one.

"How does it look?" Buzz asked, standing with his hands behind his back in the center of the large room.

"Very good," Reyas said and nodded in approval. "Now, Ramon, you must hire a good cook and housekeeper. You

take her and buy some food and meat at the market. You
know where such a one is?"

"*Si,* señor."

"Find a good cook." He closed one eye and looked con-
fidently at him.

"How much should I pay her?"

"Five dollars a week?" Reyas shrugged, uncertain what
one would cost.

"Oh, *si,* I can hire a wonderful one for that."

Reyas clapped him on the shoulder. "We want a wonderful
one." Then he handed the boy some folded money. "Keep
track and you can bring back my change."

"*Si,* señor. I will have her here and have her make supper."

"Good, I better ride back to town with Buzz and find Alphanso." The disappearance of the clerk bothered him, especially since he knew everything about his business.

"Are you satisfied then?" Buzz asked.

"It is a grand casa; we will be very proud to stay there."
Reyas gave a head toss to his latest employee and went out
the door with the banker. Finding Alphanso was his next
business.

At the livery where the clerk had stabled the two horses,
he discovered the saddlebags with the ledgers. Strange that
he would leave them on the saddle, Reyas thought, then dismissed it. Outside the stables, in the sparkling sunlight with
the saddlebags over his arm, he spoke to the stable hand.

"No, señor, I have not seen him."

Reyas set out to check the hotel and places with beds for
rent up and down the street. The head shakes they gave made
him wonder even more about the boy's absence. He might
have been queer, but always he was dependable. That's why
he had trusted him with thousands of dollars. The money
hidden in pack train shipments, Alphanso had dressed as a
peon who helped drive the burro train down there. Later, he
had set up the bank accounts with Cartwright and he had told
Reyas so much about the man. Upset about not finding him,
Reyas took the sombrero off and scratched the thin hair on
top of his head. Where could he be?

He would go ask the law. Why not? He was a businessman in this country. With money in the bank, not some crazy vaquero with dreams of being rich—he was rich, and when that boy, Ramon, looked at the accounts later on, he would tell him how rich this bastard from Old Mexico really was.

"Ah, Señor Reyas," the sheriff said and sat down after they shook hands.

It helped his name was Fernando Hidalgo, so he wasn't talking to a gringo, but one of his own.

"This boy you are looking for works for you?"

"Alphanso Domino, he is perhaps twenty."

"Is he thin? Messikin?"

"Yes, have you seen him?"

"Come with me. I may have some bad news." The man put on his black felt hat and they hurried out of the adobe jail. "This way."

They entered the undertaker parlor three doors down. Filled with questions, he hardly heard the sheriff whisper to the man what they wanted to see. Uncertain, he followed the pair and in the back room lined with fresh-smelling pine coffins, the mortician took a lid off to expose the contents. Reyas crossed himself and looked in the box.

Inside the coffin, reposed on his back, naked as a jaybird lay his clerk. He paused to look—nothing wrong with his fixtures, even dead that looked plenty adequate, that wasn't the reason he was a faggot.

"Who killed him?" He turned to the sheriff.

"We don't know much. May have been smothered under a pillow, Harvey thinks." The sheriff shifted toward the undertaker and he nodded in agreement. "That's why he has no marks on the body. Speculation, but best I know about."

"Where did they find him?"

"About dawn, but he'd been dead for a couple of hours. It was upstream under some junipers. Figure he'd been left there."

"Why? Who would do such a thing?"

"You know that boy's been to Silver City before?"

"Yes, I sent him up here on business for me."

"Thanks, Adams," the sheriff said to the undertaker. "We can handle it from here."

"I'll put the lid back. Might be some women come in here."

"Yes, good idea," the sheriff agreed and turned to Reyas. "You have some clothes for him?"

"Buy some, I'll pay for his funeral expenses," Reyas said.

"Thank you, sir."

When the man left the room, the sheriff made certain he was out of hearing before he spoke, "You know that boy was a queer?"

"Yes, but I only learned it a few days ago."

"Did he have any money on him?"

"Some, why?"

"He hung around with some unsavory *hombres* when he came up here. My deputy noticed him with them first six months ago, 'cause we watch them."

"What do they do?"

"I ain't sure, but since he's been coming around, they haven't done any work and seem to have lots of money."

"Who are they?"

"One is Bob Petts, the other is Lute McQuire."

"Bob Petts and Lute McQuire?"

"That's them. They've got a small place west of here. Now I can handle them—but first I've got to have proof it was them."

Reyas nodded. He would get proof. Then he recalled the books in the bags on his arm.

"I am certain you will arrest them," he said and thanked the sheriff, assuring the undertaker that he would be back and pay him.

"What about the funeral?"

"Find a priest, let Mr. Cartwright at the bank know and he can get me word."

"Very good. Good day, señor and Sheriff."

Hours later in his new casa, Ramon poured over the ledgers and used a pencil to make notes on a pad. Reyas sat across the table in a chair with his arms folded, wondering what the boy was doing—but he could be no help. Alphanso had made the marks, showing him thousands he said were in deposits. The fat woman, Frieda, that Ramon had hired brought them hot coffee and busied herself in the kitchen, making the evening meal. The smell of her food made Re-yas's stomach churn.

He felt satisfied the sturdy-built woman, perhaps in her fifties, knew how to please a man. He crossed his leather pants legs under the table and he leaned back, waiting.

"What news do you have?" he finally asked when the boy looked up.

"I have added all the money for your shipments from the smelter, but the accounts do not add up, señor." Ramon looked up and shook his head warily. "He deducted the money that he brought back for you to pay the salaries and expenses at the mine." The boy opened the second ledger. "But there are several thousands of dollars—I don't know?"

"How much is missing?" he asked softly.

"Twenty thousand, maybe more."

"Mother of God, you think he stole that much?"

"*Si,* señor."

"You know of these *hombres* Petts and McQuire?"

"*Si.*"

"Can we go to where they live?"

"It is a ways." He motioned to the west.

"I have horses at the stables."

"Whatever, señor."

"Frieda, you must hold our supper. We have big business," he said aloud.

She came to the doorway and nodded. "When you come back I will have it hot."

"Good," he said and stood up. "How much money do I have left?"

"A hundred thousand dollars."

He drew a deep breath of relief. "Then I have several more shipments to smelt. We can live good here, amigo. Let's go and find these two."

"They are the ones that you think may have killed him?"

Ramon asked, very serious as they hiked to the stables.

"The sheriff thinks so."

"What will we do with them?"

"Get my money back."

"But what if they fight us?"

"I have a pistol."

"I don't."

"I have another in my saddlebags. Can you shoot one?"

"*Si.*"

"Good as you are with books?" He paused to frown at the boy.

"I can shoot one."

"Don't shoot me," he said, laughed and clapped the boy on the shoulder. He would thank Maria for sending him—this one would be a keeper.

Ramon led him to the small basin in the hills. A low-walled cabin hugged a small yellow-white bluff. Beyond were some pens with horses—good, Reyas decided, that they had not fled. Squatted on his heels, he studied the lay of the land. The outhouse was back in the juniper boughs.

"How shall we do this?"

"They know you?"

Ramon shook his head.

"Take your horse and ride around, come in from the front and tell them you lost a burro. Describe it."

"Now?"

"Yes, so you know your own burro."

"It is a mare, seven years old, has pack scars, gray, has a white spot on its back—"

"Good, I'll sneak up and get the drop on them."

"Then what?"

"We will find where they have my money hidden at."

"What if they didn't—"

"Then we won't find the money. Go." He smiled at the boy. Someday that one would be powerful. He set out to skirt around and come up behind. That meant making his way unseen along the foot of the cliffs to the house.

In place, at last, he heard the boy's approach.

"Hello the house," Ramon shouted in Spanish.

Reyas smiled, pleased. The boy would be all right.

"What the hell do you want?"

"My burro is missing."

"Burro is missing. We ain't seen no burro, have you, Petts?"

"No," the second one said, coming outside.

"Hands in the sky, *hombres*!" Reyas ordered.

"Who the crap are you?" The black-bearded one he figured was McQuire because Petts, the last man out, was blonder and had little beard.

"Get their guns, Ramon," he said. "I am Alphanso's boss and I have come for the money you stole from him."

"From who?"

"You can play dumb, but you better give me the money now or you will soon regret it."

"We-we ain't got any money. Who did you say?"

"Alphanso. I know he stayed here and I know you stole his money."

"I swear, mister—"

"Listen," Reyas said to silence them. "I've been with the Apaches in the Sierra Madras. I can play their games. When an Apache gets through with you, you beg to tell him even more to stop the hurting. Get a rope, Ramon, and tie them up."

"Wait, we never—" Petts protested.

Reyas cocked his pistol, expecting some sort of a trick. The click made the younger man put his hands up.

"The money?"

"We ain't—"

"Liars! My temper is boiling. Where is it hidden?" They herded the two inside at gunpoint and Ramon found some rope.

"Tell him before he kills us," Petts said, shaking like a cold, wet dog.

"All right. It's under the floor, under the bed," McQuire said, seated in a chair with his hands bound behind him.

"Ramon, go and check." Reyas holstered his Colt and he

tied Petts's hands behind him. He stepped back and waited for the boy to move things aside. Were these two faggots too? He stepped away to watch Ramon at work.

"Part of it's here," Ramon said, straightening with a fistful of bills.

"Good."

"What're you going to do with us?"

"Smother you with a pillow like you did poor Alphanso."

"Huh—"

"Surprised I know that?"

"How?"

"Cause you just told me."

"Sumbitch—"

"Let's go to the corral." By their collars, he hoisted them to their feet. "I want to saddle your horses while he gets that money."

"Where you taking us?"

"To see Mr. Adams."

"He's the undertaker." Both men blinked at each other.

"I think so. Get moving."

The next morning at his new house, Reyas looked over at Ramon under the flickering lamplight. Both his hands held the flour tortilla loaded with meat, frijoles, cheese, tomatoes and peppers. He smiled at the pale-faced youth. "Eat up, those two we hung last night are in hell and we only lost what—"

"Three thousand, seven hundred dollars."

"*Si,* what's a few thousand anyway." Then he took a great bite.

He heard the knock on the door and Frieda ran to answer it.

"Sheriff Hidalgo," she said.

Reyas wiped his mouth on the red bandanna from around his neck. Completed, he stood up. "Come, we have much food. Eat with us, Sheriff."

The man shook his head. "I must hurry on. Those men I spoke about, Petts and McQuire—no need to worry about them anymore. Someone hung them yesterday. A rancher cut them down and brought in their bodies an hour ago.

"That's a shame. You know who did it?"

"Got notions. You and Ramon were here yesterday afternoon?"

"Except we rode out to look for a missing burro train."

"Find them?"

"No, but the driver may have found a woman somewhere." Reyas shrugged at him.

"Ah, yes, a woman." The sheriff waved and went out the door. "I must see about mine."

"Good day," Reyas said after him, saving the "I'm sorry they're dead" on the end.

"He suspects us?" Ramon whispered when the lawman was gone.

Reyas shook his head. "He's glad that justice is done. No worries. I wonder how those two seduced that dumb boy?"

"I don't understand—seduced him?" Ramon made a face.

"Never mind, we have the money." He raised his goblet of red wine. "To better days, *mi* amigo."

"Si."

15

Fresh horses and how to find them was all that occupied Durango's mind. Ever since he'd killed that worthless boy in that empty village behind them, he knew that even with the animals they had stolen in Arroyo, the two of them again needed replacements to ever outdistance the Ruralists and Slocum. Whipping his own mount and driving her horse hard ahead of him, they crossed the white alkali flats and headed for the brown foothills. Somewhere up there, a ranchero had some fresh horses for the taking. But where? In the hills perhaps—he needed to be miles out of the way of the pursuers on their heels.

She still rode straight-backed, avoiding his gaze, staring ahead. Maybe she wouldn't ever bend. Keeping her simply for his own pleasure grew less important as he glanced behind for sight of any dust in the distance. His worst fear was that when he next looked back, he would see the three of them gaining on him. Then if things got thick, she would be a valuable commodity to bargain with them over. Still, he wanted to be away from all of it. The mountain country ahead offered those possibilities and a better chance to lose them there too.

In late afternoon, he found a puddle of water in a nearly dry tank in a shady canyon. The white ghosts of barkless, dead cottonwoods lined the watercourse. Only a few still bore leaves and those were clustered around the seep. Once a lake of a several acres, the remaining water filled a spot the size of a bathtub with the dried mud scarred by wildlife and livestock tracks, many whose skeletons from starvation dotted the flats in various stages of decay.

On his knees, he refilled their skins to carry water and put them on the horses. He noticed her standing there, staring off toward the west. Did she expect those bastards to ride over that horizon any minute to save her? He had about convinced himself they would never catch him. In the hills and higher in the mountains, he would either shake or ambush them, one or the other.

From this point farther on into the bowels of the Sierra Madras, he had the advantage on them. Perhaps it would be the only way to ever escape them. He scrubbed his whisker-bristled face with the wet kerchief and let the evaporation cool some of the sun's heat radiating from his skin. Perhaps in the mountains, if he'd get high enough to reach the snow on the peaks, he could use handfuls of it to cool the insides of his galled legs and his raw, sweat-burning-a-fire crotch. He turned swiftly to see the cause of the noise when her bay shook suddenly.

"Let's ride," he said.

Without a word, she went to her horse, mounted and pushed him up the trail. Never spoke, never complained— she had to be galled too, had to be hurting, had to be half dead, but she never spoke, never said a word except to spit out her venomous talk at him when she did. Good thing she shut up; he didn't want to hear any more of that trash.

Damn, he'd rode forever and there was no end to it.

"You got any kids?" he asked.

She never answered.

"Ha, maybe I can give you some." The notion made him feel better as they rode single-file along the dried streambed. Every grass, scrub and plant was reduced to stems or dried stalks in this land of the dead. The beds of pancake cactus shriveled up like an old woman's face in a thousand wrinkles, black and twisted, as they skirted them.

Nothing was alive in this land, nothing to live for. They still needed fresh horses and someone, somewhere out there, someone had them. He looked ahead at the convoluted country they wound through. This was the way to the cooler mountains. Some small rancher was located in this country. One who held on tenaciously after his last cow died, and saved his prize horses, saved them, for he would need them in case he must leave and come back when it finally rained.

Relentlessly, he pushed all day. Sometimes forcing their spent animals to trot, sometimes to walk. The sun's fire rose up from the lifeless ground and seared their faces even underneath the shade of their hats. No escaping its blast. The bitter taste of alkali sat on his tongue, and the grit of sand scratched his sunburned eyeballs.

Then he heard a bell and told her to stop so he could ride forward and locate the sound. Perhaps the sound came from a bell mare or a cow; it was too loud for a goat. He pushed past her and rode to the next height, where he stood in the stirrups and studied the strange line of wagons.

A whole string of gypsies. More bells and their colorful rigs of red, yellow, orange and green contrasted with the bland tan of the dead desert. How many? He wasn't certain— ah, gypsies were horse traders, some even said they were horse thieves. In his pockets, he still had some of that worthless Reyas's money. Good, he would trade with them.

On fresh ponies, they would leave behind the Ruralists and Slocum. When she rode up beside him, he glanced over at her. Still a good-looking bitch; he envisioned her undressed and the thought drew saliva to his dry mouth.

"Keep you mouth shut if you want to live," he said to her and booted his horse away.

"Fuck you," she said after him.

He heard her. No matter, so long as she didn't upset them or he'd have to kill a lot of gypsies. He could do that. These people weren't *pistoleros*. He looked at their back trail one more time—nothing. Good. On fresh horses, they'd ride hard for the mountains and lose the damn Ruralists and Slocum. He took a drink of the hot water from the skin and wiped his mouth on the back of his hand. Damn gypsies would save him. He laughed aloud.

16

Slocum reined up his weary horse. He tried to judge the distance to the foothills through the wavy heat rising off the alkali flats. His tongue was too thick to let him swallow, his eye sockets drier than a burned-out cob pipe. No sign of Durango and the woman—obviously he had pushed his horses hard to have that large a space between them. No telling how far it would be to water once they reached the foothills. This drought had a rock-hard grip on the desert.

He tried to swallow and nothing was there. His throat felt like someone had taken a horseshoe rasp to it. No time for feeling sorry for himself. How did Magdellania feel? No doubt she was suffering too in the hands of such a madman. A picture of the innocents killed by the rabid dog was enough that he knew he must ride on until the horse beneath him quit, then on foot after them until he could rescue her and end that vicious killer's life.

"Slocum, how far can we go like this?" Miquel asked.

"Till we get him or die." He twisted in the saddle and looked at the two haggard men behind him.

"There should be water ahead," Ramon said in a raspy whisper.

"There should be—" Slocum agreed and booted his horse eastward. Even the dread was gone, the hot rays of the sun reflected in his face like a scorching hot iron. Nothing alive, even the water-stingy creosote bushes were dead. Leafless mesquite branches made a veil that their horses stumbled through. Fear roiled deep in his guts that at any moment his horse would fall and die. Then he would be afoot.

As the afternoon sun broiled the land and made a circuit over their sombreros, their horses' hooves shuffled in the chalky dust. First Miquel's horse quit, lay down, and no amount of swearing and kicking could make him continue.

"Best leave him," Slocum said. "We can take turns riding."

"No, go on," the man said, looking close to collapse himself.

"Grab my horn and let's go," Slocum said and dismounted. Finding his sea legs unsteady, he too clasped the horn.

"How far?" Miquel asked, shaking his head.

"We aren't leaving you," Slocum insisted.

"I would leave you."

"I doubt that. Come on," Slocum said, impatient for the man to do as he told him.

"I would—" Miquel grabbed the saddle and they began walking beside the horse. A jerky, stub-your-toe gait and then hurry-to-catch-up pace of two men half delirious with the heat and no water.

Slocum could not decide who was the worst off. Them or the horse that groaned deep in his throat. Soon Santos too was on the ground and walking to save his horse. Three lost men and two horses headed for a mirage? He hoped not. The Madras belonged in that direction, surely what he saw through the heat waves was the base of them.

No assurance there would be any water there or how far they must go—the same drought gripped most of northern Mexico. Not a single fluffy cloud for months on end even drifted over the land, let alone cried on it. Only the thought of her being in the hands of Durango forced him to toil onward.

After darkness, they reached the dry lake and only with

matches did they find the remaining water hole. Fearing their horses would colic and die they tied them and wet their shirts to wipe the animals' noses and mouths clear. Then with a canteen, they let each one slobber some of the water they poured in the sides of their mouths. A slow process in a night when it seemed that even the starlight avoided them.

Daylight came like a flannel curtain. Hungover as drunks, they awoke to see that Miquel's horse had staggered in during the night to join the others. They began to water him as they had the other two on the start, who were led over to water themselves.

Past midday, the animals had partially recovered and the men climbed in their saddles like numb stumps and headed eastward. Durango's tracks were still obvious. Slocum had seen prints of Magdellania's sandals where she had stood aside from the water and looked to the west, no doubt hoping he was coming. The notion jabbed him. No way to hurry on the animals they rode—but in the end, the turtle won the race. The results of that old fable encouraged him.

Somewhere ahead, their trails would collide. He tried to shake the bleariness from his head and eyes, but as the day wore on, it only increased. Then he thought he saw someone, but blinked in disbelief at the sight. She wore a red skirt and white blouse and was running toward him down the hillside trail. Her dark hair shone in the glaring sun. Who was she?

17

Reyas sat on the wicker rocker shifting back and forth. He took an occasional swig from the tequila bottle. The late afternoon sun was setting behind the house. His second shipment of ore had not reached Silver City yet and was long overdue. The boy, Ramon, had read aloud the man's name written in the log, Hernandos Califar. This one had taken ore to Silver City before and always came back with the receipt.

"Ramon," he called out, and the boy came out on the porch, which was shaded in late afternoon by the frame house.

"In those books, did you see the amount recorded when Califar returned the last time?"

"I can look at them, señor."

"Look."

"You suspect something?"

Reyas rose and went to stand with his shoulder against the post. Why did he not trust this Califar? Absently, he watched a trim, young gringo woman walk past. She never looked his way—

"Never mind. Come here," he said, turning to look for the boy who had the book open. "You see the señorita going down the hill?"

"Si," he said turning in the doorway.

"Good. You follow her and get all the information you can about her."

"I know her."

A small smile crept on Reyas's lips. "Who is she?"

"Felicia McCain. The storekeeper's daughter."

"Married?"

"No."

"Engaged."

"No."

"Why not?" He waited for the reply before he took another swallow.

The boy shrugged. "I have no idea. She was very smart in school."

Reyas nodded slowly as he considered the notion. Not only was she handsome-looking, but she was smart about book things. That would be what he wanted in a wife. He ran his hand over his mustache and slowly bobbed his head. He had just seen his wife-to-be.

"What does her family do?"

"They have a large mercantile store."

If they had a store, then they might owe money. And perhaps he could help the family out with his money and in turn win the hand of their daughter. He might not be able to count, but he knew that money could do many things—like earn him a young bride for his own gratitude.

"Hernandos," the boy read from the ledger. "Paid one hundred pesos for delivering the ore to the smelter."

"Which smelter?"

"Doesn't say."

"Look for another delivery?"

"Oh, here is one. Delivered to the Grimes, Simmon Great Western Mining and Smelter, Silver City, New Mexico Territory."

"Look some more. I think this Hernandos has been delivering his loads to another smelter. Him and that dead boy been splitting the money."

"You sure you can't read?" he asked, thumbing through

the pages. "Ah, here two loads back Hernandos delivered his pack train here."

"That makes how many they stole?"

"Three that do not show being delivered here. But where would they go?"

"Is it hard to sell a load of rich ore?"

"No, I guess not."

Reyas wiped his mustache and shook his head. "That little cocksucker was robbing me blind."

"How will we find this Hernandos?"

"Put a reward out. That brings the rats out of their holes."

"You want me to put one out?"

"Yes. A hundred dollars for where he is at. Here, take some money and pay for information; you will know before midnight where he is at." He put a handful of money in the boy's hand. "Ask bartenders and *putas;* for a few pesos they will even tell you what size his dick is. But we only need to know how to find him."

"*Si,* señor. You ever heard of the Hart Company?"

"No, why?"

"Alphanso paid them several sums of money."

Reyas dropped his chin in defeat. "That bugger was into it all, wasn't he?"

"I am only reporting what I have found so far."

"We will no doubt find more. Go have supper and then you find this Hernandos for me. I can handle him." He gazed off at the distant juniper-covered hillside above the house across the street. To properly court this little virgin, he would need a suit of clothes. No respectable gringo would let his daughter go out with a vaquero dressed in leather and reminding them of some border bandit. Yes, he would find a suit in the morning.

"Supper is ready, *Patrón,*" Frieda called out.

Perhaps after supper he would go see the boy's cousin. The thoughts of her great breasts made him horny for her. Yes, he needed to go see Maria.

But his real desires were for the young one; Felicia McCain was the pretty girl's name—he would know a lot more about her—soon.

18

"Good day, señor," the dark-eyed man said, coming out afoot from the wagon train.

"Howdy," Durango managed, looking at all the coal-black eyes, young and old, peering at him.

"You look very tired."

"We are," Durango said and dismounted heavily. The ring of his spur rowels sounded like bells when he stomped his heels to awaken his feet and legs. He surveyed the entire train of ten wagons.

"Need two fresh horses and some grub."

"That can be arranged," the gypsy said. "Señora, may I help you down?"

"She can get down herself," Durango said, casting a frown of suspicion at the man.

"Then may my womenfolk help her? She looks very exhausted."

Durango inhaled up his nose. He scratched the back of his neck. Then finally he nodded. "We ain't staying long."

The man waved several woman over. They chattered like magpies, rushing over as if they had been ready to gather

her. They half carried Magdellania to the wagons, oohing and aahing about her as they went.

"The food—" the man started.

"That can wait. Let's see the horses you've got." He frowned, then let a small boy have the reins to his horse and hers to hold.

"My name is Frechez."

"Durango," he said, preoccupied with keeping an eye out for anything threatening coming from the wagons. Several men sat about smoking in their midday camp—looked harmless enough—still, he had no plans on being taken by surprise. One move out of them oily-looking bastards and they'd go to hell in a hail of his gunfire.

"See the red horse?" Frechez asked, pointing to a shiny, small horse.

It would do to carry her. Had lots of barb blood in its veins from the looks of its dish face and small ears. "How much?"

"Thirty dollars."

"Too high."

The man shrugged and pointed to a large blue roan. Branded and scarred, one ear was cropped half off, the other split. His long mane and the way his hips sloped down told Durango this was a tough critter. This gelding had been a lot of places. He walked close enough to check him for splits or ringbone. Satisfied the roan had turned smooth mouth, he clapped his hands. The horse jerked back and spun around. Careful to see how the animal moved, he watched him go chase another from the precious grain spilled in spots on the ground for them. Those two would do.

"How much for the pair?"

"Sixty dollars."

"High, aren't you?"

"I have more horses like the ones you rode in upon. They are cheaper."

"Fifty in gold."

"Fifty-five."

"Tell that boy to bring them horses over. I ain't got time

to argue. Get them saddles switched and we're riding on."
He glanced back to the west—nothing. But at last, he had
the animals to outdistance them on. A smile set in his full
lips and he drew out his purse; carefully he counted out the
money from the coins. Some *puta* in Fronteras had taught
him how to count and sign his name.

"You want food?"

"I'd take some jerky. You got some?"

"Yes, but we could feed you."

"Jerky'll be fine. Tell that bitch to get over here. Soon as
we get saddles on them we're leaving."

"*Si*, señor."

"Tell her to get her ass over here pronto too." He scowled
at the camp and undid the cinches, taking quick glances at
them in case she'd roused them up about him kidnapping
her. She better get over there. He jerked the cinch tight on
the roan, knowing the horse had blown himself up. A sharp
toe to his gut and he finished cinching him, then he turned
to the chestnut. Cute horse, plenty big enough for her. Never
could tell about them barbs, size had nothing to do with them.
A lot of bottom—he jerked the bridle hard when it tried to
dance and set it down, tossing on the wet blanket, then the
hull she rode. Cinched, he turned and she went past him.

In a bound, she was aboard and had the horse checked
close. The pony danced in a circle and he smiled.

"Good to be on a real horse, ain't it?"

She never answered him, but looked to the taller hills to
the east.

"Go that way," he said and took a fistful of jerky from the
gypsy. "See ya," he said over his shoulder and followed the
single-footing chestnut up the flat for the next range.

Their fresh horses reinforced his confidence. Then he
looked back to the west—good, no sign of them.

19

"Señor, she asked that I warn you. She says, he will ambush you if you follow him in the mountains." The woman, out of breath, bent over and put both hands on her knees.

"Have they gone on?" Slocum asked, looking at the hill she came from.

"Yes—she was—very worried—about you."

"We are very worried for her, señora." He dismounted.

"But she says he will . . ."

"These men I ride with are Ruralists. He won't kill all of us."

The woman fought back tears. Obviously her mission was falling on deaf ears and the notion upset her.

"We need fresh horses. Can your people spare them?"

She nodded in defeat.

"That's why we hurry."

With a shrug, she gathered her skirt and started up the hill. "Follow me."

Slocum nodded to the other two and they rode after him. It would be Magdellania's way to tell them not to follow— a martyr acted like that and she fit the role. Someone needed to stop this killer and they were the closest to doing it. Perhaps with fresh horses, they'd soon ride him in the ground somewhere ahead. Just so they did it before he hurt her any worse.

The gypsies found them three sound horses. The women fed them while their saddles were switched. Daring not to sit upon the ground, for fear they would never get up again, they stood stiff and ate from the fine china bowls and silverware. Food rich in spice, the tender chunks of lamb floated in a tomato-vegetable and barley stew.

"Gracias," both Ruralists said again as women brought them fresh bread to sop in the juices.

"She is your woman?" the woman who called herself Carmen asked Slocum.

"We're friends. A bad man named Reyas had her husband killed and I came along after that."

She nodded she heard him. "He is running from you. He wouldn't even eat."

Slocum agreed. "Why we must push on and catch them."

"May God be with you, amigos," she said.

"We can pay for the food—"

"No, we want her safe. I hated there were no men in this camp strong enough to stop him."

"He's a bad killer."

"We saw that in his eyes. Needs no reason, does he?"

"None. He's left a trail of dead ones. You're lucky."

"But we have no pride," she said under her breath.

"Yes, you do. You are a proud, clean people in a land of dust and no water."

"It is hard," she said and smiled at his words that he considered her people clean. She stood a little straighter. "People without a land must be proud."

"Gracias," he said and tipped his hat to her.

"You never said your name?"

"Slocum."

"I thought she meant you came slow. God be with you, Slocum. I will burn a candle for you when I get to the next mission."

"We will need it."

The people from the camp clapped their hands at them as they rode away. With fresh horses and water, they pressed the tracks he left them. Riding into the mountains made Slocum feel better. Even without rain, springs seeped out of the granite and the once-mighty rivers usually had spring holes. He looked behind and saw the first teaser clouds coming from the faraway Gulf of California.

Not fat, towering thunderstorms, but it was only midday and they were headed for collision with the peaks ahead of them. His tight shoulders let go of a little of their fiddle-string tightness. Maybe if Carmen burned enough candles she could even bring moisture in to this thirsty land.

The three pushed on. They found a small pile of horse droppings still with heat in them, according to Santos, who dismounted and squeezed one apple to test it. The way grew steeper and the vegetation turned to brown live oak and junipers, giving a heady smell in the air of evergreen. Small birds flitted in the branches and that meant water existed close by.

They spooked a herd of javelinas that ran off the mountain at the sight of them. Not daring to risk taking a shot, Slocum looked at his supper rush off into a steep canyon in a series of short barks, rolling rocks loose in their flight.

Then further on they watched a small flock of wild turkeys eye them suspiciously, then walk away. No sight of Durango and the woman, but their tracks showed they had moved through ahead of them at a trot across this portion. The sun over their shoulders dropped into the Pacific in a blaze of oranges and purples marked by the clouds that ran from one horizon to the next.

"We better make camp," Slocum said. His tired eyes scoured the slopes above them cast in the last golden light of day. "No moon tonight either."

The others agreed and dropped heavily from their saddles. Then Santos said, "Listen."

Off to the north came the sounds of falling water. They ran over to peer deep in the canyon and silver water flashed deep in the cut.

"No way to get a horse down there without riding around," Slocum said.

"I'd go down there and take a bath," Santos said.

"Me too."

"Hell, let's hobble these ponies and go down there," Slocum said, as game as they were for the chance to wash away some of the layers of grit.

Twilight still held the mountains when they hurriedly undressed and each took a pool between the rocks to cup water over themselves. To cool the places like under their arms galled by the sweat and dirt of the ride. Then standing straddle-legged, Slocum washed the raw places between his legs. The cool water first burned him as the body salt was washed into the exposed cuts and creases. At last, seated in the small pool with the stream rushing over his legs, he felt for the first time in days refreshed.

In the growing darkness, he washed his underwear, pants and shirt, recalling the bare-breasted women of the village laughing and gossiping as he rode by them. Clothing hung to dry on some limbs, he went back to sit and again cool his sore butt and privates in the water.

"Ah, amigo," Santos said. "Today we ate with silverware on fine china, tonight we are washed and clean again. If we had some women—we'd be complete, no?"

"Your fist will have to be the fine one that you dance with tonight," Miquel said and laughed.

"I could have taken me a gypsy back there," Santos said, sounding full of regret.

"Ha," Miquel said. "That is why they even moved their sheep to the other side of the camp when they saw us coming."

Slocum laughed, and dressed in his still damp underwear and carrying his handgun and clothing, he began his trek up the steep wall that they had descended. "I heard those sheep saying, 'Baaad Ruralists!' "

"Real bad," Miquel agreed, starting up hill after him.

Out of breath, Slocum strung his clothing on a juniper and in the starlight saw the other two coming up from the canyon.

"Have some jerky," Santos said.

Slocum agreed, taking what the man handed him, and listened to the far-off howl of the red wolf. Then another answered it. The deep-throated cry made goose bumps on the back of his arms. Tomorrow they would be rested and catch up with this dog they hounded—Magdellania, we are coming.

20

"Ah, Hernandos," Reyas said, the big Colt in his hand and cocked.

The man looked ready to make a move—then trapped, he settled down in surrender. Reyas shoved the muzzle in his face.

"You think I am stupid?"

Hernandos shook his head, staring at the weapon.

"Tie him up," Reyas ordered and Ramon rushed in with the rawhide to quickly thrust the man's hands behind him.

"There. Now you tell me about the deal you and that queer made." Reyas holstered the Colt and drew out the skinning knife from his belt in the candlelight. Acting very intent on it, he tested the edge on his thumb. "You aren't saying much."

"I don't know what you speak about."

"Where did you take the ore?"

"Where Alphanso told me to take it."

"Not to where the rest of them went?"

"I only did—"

"Señor," the boy cried out at some discovery. "Here is a receipt for two thousand dollars from Southwest Smelter."

"Two thousand dollars, huh? Where's the money, huh, amigo?"

"I don't—"

In a flash, Reyas grabbed the man's ear in his left hand and began close to his skull, cutting downward with the sharp blade. Hernandos screamed like a woman when he sliced off the whole ear flush to his head and then held it close to the packer's face.

"You don't hear so good from that ear, no?"

"Oh, no," Hernandos moaned and leaned forward as blood began to darken that side of his face and drip off his beard.

"You won't die that easy. What did you and that little bastard do with my money? Talk and talk fast or the other ear comes off."

"He said you would never miss a shipment 'cause you could not read. I promise you, I had to do as he said—or else—"

"Or what? He would tell the others what you did."

"You know—" Hernandos blinked in disbelief.

"You like to suck off boys too?"

A visible nod and the packer bent forward; he said nothing more.

"Tell me what he did with the money."

"Hid it. I guess. There was plenty. I brought him three times that much." He indicated the receipt in the pale-faced Ramon's hand.

"What about this time?"

"They wouldn't pay me. Said that he was dead and they owed no one."

"Who are these men would not pay you?" Reyas looked at Ramon who nodded that he knew them. Good enough, they would collect that money too.

"Ones run that smelter. One's called Jenks," the sobbing Hernandos managed.

"You know them?" he asked the boy. When Ramon said yes, Reyas reached for the pistol in the holster hanging over the chair. With it in his hand, he pressed it to the bloody side of the man's head and pulled the trigger. The shot knocked him and the chair over. In the strong haze of gun smoke, Reyas cut his hands loose while the packer's feet and legs thrashed in death's throes. Then he pressed the gun in the dead man's hand, putting his finger through the guard.

"Shame after he cut off his own ear for penitence, he couldn't stand it anymore and shot himself." He walked over and took a razor from beside a chipped enamel wash pan. Then he bloodied the handle and blade from the victim's own source, then he rose and placed it open on the table beside the cut-off ear.

"I found two sacks of coins," the boy said, hefting them from a pack on the floor.

"Good. If he has any money on him, leave it and they won't suspect it was robbery." He took one of the heavy canvas sacks and smiled. "See, I told you pay a *puta* and you can learn it all. Now I want you to arrange it so I can meet this woman, Felicia McCain."

"What of that man he mentioned and the money at the other smelter they owed you?"

"We better go see them, before the word gets out."

"I'll locate them and collect it for you. Should I put this money in the bank?"

"No, we may need it. Hide it in my trunk at the casa and lock it."

"*Si, patrón.* Should we blow out the candle?"

He shook his head. Then he used a broom to wipe out their tracks back to their horses under the starlight that sparkled overhead. Among the tracks of the burros, they would be hard to trace. They rode back to his house.

So many crooks in New Mexico. He shook his head imagining how many had tried to steal his money. First the pair that killed Alphanso. Then his own trusted clerk had been stealing with the packer Hernandos. It was a whole network of thieves in this place. But him and this boy would soon have all his losses recovered that they could and he would concentrate on being a rich gringo rancher with a wife. A young one of fair skin. Yes and many little Reyases running about the place—ah, he would be the *patrón*.

21

"You smell like a pig," she said and shoved him away. "Go take a bath."

Durango's brain flared like gunpowder in a pan on a blunderbusts. Then he exploded and reached for her, but she shrugged off his hands like they were nothing. The insolent glare in her eyes forced him to consider her again.

"You want my body, you go take a bath. No woman appreciates a stinking boar hog." She drew back her head and shook it.

"When I do come back, you better pucker your asshole, cause I'll give you a screwing that you won't forget."

"When you're clean."

"I'll be clean. You better get ready to choke on my pecker."

"Clean, we will see it."

He tossed aside his sombrero and began to strip off his shirt, headed for the streambed. En route he undid his gun belt. Why, he'd show her—he unbuckled his belt with a jerk in the starlight and toed off his boots. He glanced back as she came gathering up his clothing in her arms. Soon she had a pile in her arms and he turned to let her see his great tool in his fist.

With a nod of approval, she gathered up his boots and added them to her armful. He went off into the knee-deep water and began splashing the water on himself. He'd show her. She'd see what a stallion he was—what the hell?

Where was she going with them horses? He rushed out of the stream and searched for his pistol as she rode the chestnut and led his blue roan away into the inky night. Holy mother of God, she took his pistol too. Cold chill bumps began to prick his back and the truth of the situation began to settle like a hard rock in his gut. Tricked by that bitch Magdellania. He listened to the red wolves howl on the cool night wind that swept his bare skin.

Run or wait? Rurales never took prisoners—he bent over in pain as a sharp stub jabbed his sole. No way to even hang himself.

"Damn you, Magdellania! May a thousand curses make your life one of barren misery!" he shouted at the night.

He felt for his privates and realized how shrunken his scrotum had become. Then the cold knife of fear began to probe him: no gun, no knife, no clothes—no chance. He shook away his fears—he would hide in the brush with a club and ambush one of them before they killed him. They would never get Durango.

If he wasn't afraid, why was he standing there pissing on his own bare feet? Then the red wolf howled again, only closer. Bastards, bad as Slocum and the Ruralists—Reyas, where are you? You sumbitch, you got me into this. May you never have a hard-on again!

When he heard the horses coming, Slocum put on his boots and, with his pistol in hand, waited. He was joined by a sleepy Santos, who asked him who was coming. They blocked the trail, guns ready.

"I need help!" she shouted, reining the excited horse to a halt.

Santos captured the roan and held him while Slocum caught her bridle.

"We can help you, Magdellania," Slocum said, with a sigh of relief. "How far away is he?"

"I'm—" She swallowed hard. "Not certain, but he has no clothes, no gun, no horse."

Slocum turned to the other two in the starlight and they nodded in approval.

Like a gentleman, Santos bowed at his waist in his one-piece underwear and laughed when he straightened. "Sorry we weren't dressed for your coming, señora."

"It doesn't matter," she said and collapsed into Slocum's arms.

He held her tight to him and savored her closeness. In response, she hugged him tight and he could feel her shaking. The ordeal had been hard on her, but in the end she had even outfoxed the rabid one.

"You two can stay here," Santos said to the two of them as they dressed. "We can handle him."

"Don't forget that a denned animal is always more desperate than a free one," Slocum warned them.

"*Si,* we won't take any chances," Miquel promised.

"Boys, I came this far?" He looked them over in the flannel light of sunup.

"You have been a great leader or we'd never gotten to here. We will ride back with you, if you wish, Slocum."

"Good enough," he said and went to the fire where she was making them some beans.

"Save us some," Santos said and the two rode up the mountain.

She straightened from her stirring. "It has been a long time."

"Since we lay in your hammock?" He blew the steam from his coffee.

"Yes. Many times I regretted we had not made love."

"I worried so much about your safety."

She wrinkled her nose. "You chased him so hard he never had a chance to do anything."

"I'm glad for you."

"It would make no difference. I regretted we had not—"

"Guess we can do it anytime—" He dropped his gaze to his coffee and watched the steam swirl in the gentle breath of the wind. When he looked up, she had her blouse half off, exposing her round, firm breasts. Then, visibly shaking and trembling in the first light, she cleared the garment over her head.

"How about now?" she asked.

"Yes." He swallowed hard and began to toe off his boots. He watched her run to the chestnut horse and soon she whipped open a woven rug to lay upon the ground. Their bedstead complete, she undid the ribbons that held on her skirt.

"I am not very clean," she cautioned him.

"There's always time for a bath," he said and swept her into his arms. Mouths melted and they soon became one demanding body. She pulled him to the blanket and scooted underneath him, raising her legs for him to part her gates.

When he began his entry, she threw back her head and cried aloud. Her back arched, she clawed with her fingernails at his shoulders for more. Then her legs crossed over his and she raised up to meet his thrusts. Contractions inside her walls began to wring him out. Soon the head of his dick grew so swollen that she began to moan in pleasure and the fire rose from his balls. Like a cannon charge, he came and she pushed her body to him, then she went limp underneath him.

She awoke from her faint. Weaving her head from side to side, she mumbled something about "wonderful," then pulled him down to softly kiss his chest again and again in gratitude.

"Now I know what I have missed—oh, so dumb." She closed her eyes. "Wish now I could wash."

"Down in the canyon," he said with a head toss.

"Let's go."

He glanced up the mountain as they stood up. "Better take our clothes. Them two might be back."

"Sure," she said and bumped her hip into him.

"Good," he said, wondering how those two were doing tracking down a naked bandit.

Durango stood in the stunted pines. His soles ached from the thorns and rocks. Out of breath, he checked the sun—midday. If he could find anyone—steal their horse and go—anything. He wiped his bristled mouth. He was sweating and his body skin felt cold. Nothing made any sense. Then, finding a sharp stick underfoot, he rushed forward three steps before regaining his balance.

Something heavy struck his back and sent him facedown into the litter of dry pine needles. He heard the report of the faraway rifle as he fought to get up. The knife in his chest felt deep. When he glanced down, he saw a hole the size of a double eagle where the bullet had torn out of his chest. He plastered the wound with handfuls of dirt and pine needles, then gained his feet.

Another piece of hot lead tore through his gun arm, and he stared in disbelief as the shattered elbow hung useless at his side. He whirled to see his enemy and the next bullet knocked him back two steps, but he recovered and glared at them—they couldn't kill Durango. He was invincible, but the flurry of their next bullets soon smashed him to the ground.

He looked up at the cottony clouds. Was it thunder he heard? Uncertain, he watched the towering column overhead. Then he could hear them close by cursing him. One of the Ruralists grasped a handful of his hair and with a big knife began cutting off his head. It went dark.

22

"What do you mean the Ruralists got Durango?" he whispered, looking around to be certain that no one saw him talking to this former employee, Torga.

"They took his head to Fronteras and put it on a spike in the square with the rest of the men they shot and beheaded at the cantina."

"How did you escape?"

"I got away before they shot the others at the cantina and walked out of the canyon."

"I owe you some money?"

The man nodded.

"My clerk is gone. Here, have a few pesos. But don't get drunk here. The sheriff doesn't need to know anything." He handed him the money. "Don't get drunk and cause me any trouble," he hissed after Torga as he left the porch.

He had little time for the likes of his former employee. This day he was to have supper with the McCain family. The new suit was supposed to be completed—the Lebanese tailor promised on his life to have it completed by midday. Too early for him to go yet and check on it. This boy, Ramon, had become invaluable. He had collected from those thieves at the Southwest Smelter. He had even arranged for Reyas's invitation to this meal.

Yes, Ramon had learned that her father could use a partner. His store business was growing fast as Silver City and more towns to the north needed stores. There was always the need for more money to buy merchandise, the cost of freight from the railhead—perhaps they needed their own wagons and teams. The boy had such wonderful plans and spoke of more riches from those things. For Reyas, all this business was enough to boggle his mind; still, if it allowed him to marry that girl—then it would be excellent.

Carefully, he had spied upon her. Heard her laughter in the company of two other girls. The sound made his heart race as he stood back in the shadows beside the tin building, listening to her a short distance away. Her voice was so melodious. Would his accented English bother her? No way that he could ever be like the boy and speak the second tongue that good. Mother of God, help me take her for my bride. Ready or not, he was going to see if that heavier-accented man than him had his suit completed. This day he would become a gringo and not the damn vaquero from Mexico.

"I am going to see about the clothes," he shouted for the boy's sake and his housekeeper.

In long strides, he headed downhill. Upset to the point of screaming with all the waiting, he tried to rationalize how to control himself. Then he thought of Maria and her big ass. With a check at the sun time, still mid-morning, he decided a quick turn in the bed with her might settle this anxiousness that possessed him.

He crossed the log footbridge over the creek and shooed away the curious goats who came forward to meet him. Fighting-stock hens and their little chicks scratched in the yard. He stopped at the back door, put the sombrero on his shoulders with the rawhide cord at his throat and peeked inside.

"Ah, it is you," she said and looked up from her corn grinding with the rock and metate. She reached for a cloth

and wiped the beads of sweat from her face as she rose.
"Whew, good to see you."

"You have work to do?"

She shrugged. "Someday. What do you need?"

"You alone?"

"You see anyone else?" She crossed her ample arms over
the full breasts.

He looked around. "Want to go to bed?"

She wrinkled her nose. "It is daylight."

"So?"

He shook his head. "What difference does that make?"

"I like to have a fandango, drink, and dance, then go to
bed with a lover." But her look soon softened and he guessed
she was only acting hard-to-get. No one wanted to be like a
puta and jump in bed whenever they jingled change in their
pocket.

"I will go buy a bottle," he offered.

"No, I have some good red wine."

"I can replace it."

"Ah, you are a rich man. You can afford the best. I like
that diamond you sent me, but where could I wear it?"

Her words made him uneasy. He didn't want everyone to
know the extent of his wealth; someone might try to rob him
and be disappointed, for he carried little money on his person.

She looked around and wet her lips, then she held out her
arms. In a flash, he was inside them, holding her face in his
hands and kissing her like a man starved to death. Yes, yes,
this would settle his boiling blood.

In a moment, he began to fondle her melon-sized breasts.
Then he bunched the material up and got on his knees to
suck on the huge, pointed, dollar-sized nipples like a man
dying of thirst. Her hands were at the back of his head clutch-
ing him to them and she was crying out songs of her pleasure.

In minutes, she lay on top of the table with her skirt wad-
ded up on her belly. He ripped open his pants to uncover his
dick, and with it in his fist he aimed his throbbing sword for
the pinkish slit between her wide-apart ham-like thighs. In-

side her at last, he began to hump hard until his pelvis was hard against her. The aching in his buttocks was so consuming he knew he must find the depth of her.

She cried out loud in pleasure with, "More. More."

Then he knew his shaft would soon explode and pushed into his deepest point so the head of his dick rammed into her stiff cervix. Multicolored fireworks exploded in his brain, he felt knives pierce his testicles and the depleting effort drained all the strength from his body.

She raised up on her elbows with sleepy-looking eyes. "You are even better than a fandango."

"So are you," he said, wiping off his slimy peter with her rag.

"Where are you going?" she asked, sitting up and combing her hair back with her fingers. Her thick legs still apart, she sat up, but made no move to cover them with her skirt.

"To get my suit."

"Don't stay away so long," she said and then laughed as he finished pulling up his pants.

"I won't." He smiled at her and winked. All the pretty young women and daughters of the miners he took at will when he ran the mines, none were as good as this fat-assed one. Why? They never had sex just for the pleasure of it—didn't know how. He enjoyed them, but nothing like he savored her.

He dug out some coins and put them on the table. "Buy some good wine for the next time."

"Real good wine," she said and came off the table one side at a time. The skirt finally fell and blocked his looking at her bare legs.

From the door, he put his sombrero back on and waved good-bye to her. He hurried to the shop, settled some, but was still anxious to see what he would look like in a mirror as a gringo.

The little man held out the clothing, piece by piece, as he dressed. Then when the pants were on, the tailor gave them a critical look and stuck his fingers over the waistband and jerked on them.

"Dey fits, no?"

"Yes," he said, remembering not to say *si*. They felt itchy. Lots of air around his legs compared to his leather pants. The hairs on his legs felt like they were coming unsprung and he wanted to shake all over like a horse did after a long ride. Then the collarless white shirt: he liked the feel of the cloth. The man put on the celluloid collar and then a tie, demonstrating how to make the knot.

"See, wrap, then over, under and pull down. Very simple."

"Sure," Reyas agreed, but decided the boy could do that for him. Up, over and around and through sounded too complicated for him.

He held the suit coat out for Reyas to put his arms in it. He stuck one arm in, then the second and pushed out his chest to look at himself in the large oval mirror.

At last he was a gringo, no longer a vaquero from the brush. Ah, if only those *bastardos* that knew him in the village as a boy could see him now. They would never believe how well he had done for himself. He turned sideways and yes, he looked very *americano*.

"You will want another suit to go riding in?" the man asked.

He nodded in approval. Still examining his image, he ran his tongue around the edges of his sharp teeth, a taste of her still lingering in his mouth. *Ah, Maria—you saved my life today*. In this fine suit he would go and meet his wife-to-be.

"Send this suit to my house at once and the boy will pay you. And yes, make me a riding suit." He quickly undressed and put on his familiar clothing, feeling at once more at ease.

"It will require a few days?"

"Get it done."

"Yes, sir, yes, sir, Señor Reyas."

He held up a finger and shook his head. "No more señor. I am Mr. Reyas."

"Oh, yah, Mr. Reyas."

He nodded, satisfied, and put on his stiff-brimmed sombrero. He stood in the noontime sun before the shop and watched the vehicles and riders go past. He wondered what he must do about Torga. Sooner or later the man would talk or try to blackmail him out of money. He needed to make a complete cut with his past.

He began to scout the cantinas. He found him sitting on the ground with a bottle in the shade of a building. Certain that he was not being observed, Reyas eased around the side and approached the man.

"Hey," Torga said with a slur in his voice that betrayed his state of intoxication.

"Hey yourself, *mi* amigo. Let's go down by the river." Reyas checked around again to be certain that no one was close by or watching them.

"Sure," Torga said and struggled to get to his feet. "I couldn't believe it when they tell me that Durango's head was on a pike at Fronteras. He was such a tough *hombre*." He shook his head in deep concentration over the matter. "My God, he was the meanest man I ever knew." With a pained expression he looked up at Reyas as if to question him. "Those bastards killed him. The damn Ruralists and that gringo scout with them."

"We should have shot that scout."

"Yeah, that one called Slocum."

Reyas nodded and made his way through the willows. The gurgle of water over the rocks was close at hand. Was anyone in sight? He slipped the sombrero on his shoulder and glanced back to see the man tilting the bottle up for another deep drink. He parted the willow screen and saw nothing but the sparkling water.

"Let's get a drink of water," he said and dropped to his knees on the sandy gravel.

"Sure—" Torga agreed. He knelt beside him and bent over. When he did, Reyas forced his face down into the water. With a knee pressed into Torga's back, he enforced his action. The man struggled, bubbles escaping from both sides of his head, which looked distorted in the clear waters. His struggling was to no avail, for both of Reyas's hands held his face under and the weight of Reyas's knees on his back was too much to throw off. Soon no air came out and the man's body grew limp underneath him.

Reyas listened to the birds chirping in the willows, still holding him down. At last, he rose, and used a stick to wipe out the signs of his rawhide knee boots in the sand. One less to speak out against him.

Fifteen minutes later, he sat on the front porch of his casa in the rocker. This night he would meet his future wife. The recall of her melodious laughter made him smile as the chair's runners drummed on the porch flooring.

23

Slocum lay sprawled on his back in the hammock. High above him a noisy Mexican mockingbird scolded him. A week of rest and he felt satisfied to stay forever in the deep canyon with Magdellania. Things were going smooth at the mine. The co-op was working.

"Señor?"

He looked up and saw the face of Cruz.

"Sorry to come at such a bad time. You are resting, but I need some advice and perhaps some help."

Slocum dismissed his concern with a wave and swung his stockinged feet over the side. Sitting on the edge, he combed his hair back with his fingers. "Have a seat on that stool. What did you need?"

"We need someone to go to Silver City who speaks English and can make arrangements for a smelter to work our ore. The ones in Mexico are not good and they are not honest."

"They speak Spanish up there."

"No, señor, we need a representative that knows many things. We have little or no education, no skills at such things and the ore is fast piling up at the mine."

"You need to hire a bookkeeper."

"*Si,* that's what we need. But we don't know of any."

"I am not a bookkeeper."

The man nodded. "But you know of such things and how they work."

"You want me to make a deal with the smelters up there?"

"Reyas had such a deal, we know, and he put his money in the bank up there."

"You will need some of the money back here?"

"Yes, but we will need as you say a bookkeeper too. There are supplies we must buy and also money for the workers' pay."

"All right, I will ride to Silver City and make a deal and look for a bookkeeper. He will want a good salary to come here."

"How much?"

"Two hundred pesos a month, a place to live in, a house-keeper."

"Oh," the man said, relieved. "We can afford that."

"So if I find a bookkeeper I should bring him back?"

"*Si.*"

"I need to shoe my horses before I can ride there."

"No, we will take them and have them shod for you. How much money will you need?" Cruz asked.

"Some."

"How much?"

"Two hundred pesos."

"No problem. I will have the money for you in the morning. We will prepare two pack horses with supplies."

"Send along with me two of your young men who will later take the pack trains up there so they will know the way and how to do business."

"Very good idea. When will you leave?"

Slocum considered his situation. A few more days of peace in her company and then he could ride out on that big blue roan horse that the two Ruralist insisted was to be his to keep. He nodded to himself. "Day after tomorrow?"

"Excellent, señor." Cruz excused himself and left Slocum

to stretch the stiffness from his shoulders. He looked up to see her bringing them tea on a tray.

"Too late," he said to explain Cruz's departure. "He has business."

"So you will go up there to Silver City?" She placed their tray on a stool and pulled another up to join him.

"To set up the smelting deal and find a bookkeeper for them."

"What if Reyas is there? He will remember you." She handed him a steaming mug.

"Lots of people remember me."

"But not all will want to kill you."

He felt the moisture forming from the hot tea on his upper lip and blew across the surface. "I'll not give them a chance. You wish to go along?"

She stood up and looked to the west. He sipped the sweet tea and waited for her to answer. Twice, she glanced aside at him, then each time quickly turned back as if she was appraising her future.

"Yes," she said at last. "I wish to join you on this journey."

"You know I might not be able to come back here?"

"I understood that the first time you came to my casa."

"Shame—" He paused and then shook his head. "But my life is never settled."

"One or two weeks or whatever we have been together I have enjoyed each hour."

"Oh, the pleasure is all mine."

She scooted her skirt under her and sat down. With the cup in her hand, she raised it in a toast. "To a successful trip."

They clinked them together and he smiled at her.

"I must go to the chapel and light candles for our success," she said.

Yes, they probably would need God on their side, he agreed. The tea drew the saliva in his mouth; he closed his eyes, filled with the dread that he must soon leave this Garden of Eden and the wonderful Magdellania.

• • •

The two packers selected were named Bronco and Cyd. Bronco was the burly-chested one and his deep voice carried like a ship's horn. Cyd was slender built and had few words. Both looked, to Slocum, to be under twenty and rode good saddle mules. Magdellania rode the chestnut, frisky and ready to single-foot. He chose the larger blue roan to pack him over the mountains and desert. Three good-size mules carried their supplies and bedrolls. His entourage set out from the mine camp in the early morning twilight to the cheers of the mine crew and their families.

The way out of the canyon was a long pull, single file. On the roan, Slocum rode at the head of the column and Cyd drove the three pack mules on the end of the train.

At last in the pass, he let the cool wind sweep his sweaty face for a moment and gazed across at the other towering mountains. Clouds in the south promised an afternoon monsoonal shower—an usual happening since they'd returned. Still, it would require many soaking rains to ever restore this land from the two years of drought, even in the mountains where small amounts of moisture had fallen in that period.

The well-defined trail wound northward on a bench in the range and Bronco rode up to ask him questions.

"The way to the border is this clear?"

"Most of the way. You will have to space the watering place and without much graze left up here, you will need to grain your pack animals, so some will have to carry that feed."

Bronco agreed and rode back to discuss the ideas with Cyd. She came up beside Slocum as they skirted the dull pine timber showing the effects of the drought too.

"One could get lost up here."

"On purpose or otherwise?"

"I mean if you can't stay in the canyon?"

He looked to the west and could see for a hundred miles across the hazy desert far below them to the distant horizon marked in sawtooth purple mountains. No way to explain it all to her, that he had no place on the earth to throw his hat down for long. Sooner and later they always came for him.

• • •

The third day they reached a sleepy mountain village. Their animals' shoes rang like bells on the stone-paved street. Single-file, they crossed the arched bridge and drew some serious gazes. Two renegade mountain Apaches in knee-high rawhide boots and breech clothes eyed them with interest. Their slitted eyes were like those of a diamondback rattler— remnants of Geronimo's last band that still moved through the mother mountains like campfire smoke on a soft wind. Slocum wondered if he knew either of them, but they turned and were gone into the shadows before he could examine them.

"Will we stop here?" Bronco called out.

"For some food," he said and nodded, tossing his head to the cantina ahead. The rich smoke of oak and mesquite filled the air and Slocum recalled the fine *cabrito* they served. Fat, young goats roasted over the flavorful smoke.

"Ah!" a fat waitress shouted and ran to hug him when he entered the courtyard. "You return, *mi* gringo."

"Magdellania, meet Lupe," he said and waved his sombrero at the mustached man in an apron standing in the back. "What's cooking?"

"Fat goat, pig, we have plenty of both." The man showed his even teeth and came forward to shake his hand. "You stay away too long." He nodded to her and the two boys. "You bring hungry ones with you?"

"For your great food, yes."

"Come sit in the shade," Lupe offered and showed them a table with benches on the patio.

Several dark eyes shifted to observe them as they took places, but the curious soon went back to their own food and he felt satisfied they were no threat. Lupe brought the wine and the mugs were filled with the juice of the vine. Wooden bowls of well-browned meat filled the table and men reached with their knives to slice some of this and that. Their lips turned greasy and tongues licked the last flavor from them.

Lupe returned with a stack of white flour tortillas and leaned over close to his ear. "Men were here a few days ago and asked about you," she whispered in his ear and then made a show to kiss his cheek.

"You know them?"

"They ride for that Peralta bitch."

He nodded and thanked her softly. To dismiss Magdellania's look of concern, he shook his head to her to postpone speaking about the subject.

"How many?" he asked Lupe before she left.

"Less than the last time. Maybe five this time."

"They must be getting weary."

"They looked rode out to me," the woman said and then curled her lip. "She has the same old dog leading them. I think when the rest quit, he will still look."

"Matta—Matamoris?"

Lupe nodded. "Same old dog."

"Gracias."

She shook her head in disapproval and went to kiss a white-bearded vaquero seated at a nearby table with some boys who were dressed like him. The older man's eyes glowed and he grinned big at her attention.

"Ah, Lupe!" he shouted.

"Ah, Varga!" she said and clapped her hands, hurrying off for more food.

Slocum paid for their meal while the packers went to check the cinches. When Magdellania rejoined them, they mounted up and headed *norte.*

"How many of your enemies were there?" she asked, pushing in close as they rode past the small farms that lined the river and were watered by small acequias. Crops of corn, alfalfa, melons and beans grew profusely behind stone wall fences. Then they rode by grazing flocks of sheep and goats tended by children and old men with dogs.

"Perhaps none," he said finally to her as he looked over their back trail.

"Matta who?" she asked.

"An old foreman who knows lots about cows and mountains."

"He looks for you?"

"He works for her." Slocum nodded and visualized the naked Evon standing with her bare feet apart on the tile floor. Hands on her hips, pear-shaped breasts hard as rocks. A line ran down her muscle-tight belly that dissected her deep navel and the indention went to the dark pubic bush. Her rich olive skin turned a polished oak brown in the shade of the room. The red highlights tinting her curly black hair—only the devil could have made such a woman.

"What does she mean, *bitch*?" Magdellania asked, breaking his daydream.

"Spoiled child," he said. Spoiled by her older father, she grew up motherless—she died at Evon's birth.

"She has a name?"

"Evon Peralta."

Magdellania shook her head. "Never heard of her."

"Just as well."

"This Matamoris is looking for you because she wants you?"

He nodded mildly. "Wants me dead."

"Why is that?"

"If she can't have me, then no one else should."

She looked to the west and nodded. "Then she is a bitch."

24

"Señor Reyas, my daughter, Felicia," the man graying at the temples introduced her.

He made a bow and took her hand to kiss. When he looked into her eyes they were closed with her innocence and a small blush that brought color to her peach-colored cheeks.

"My pleasure, young lady. You have your mother's handsome looks."

He then bowed for her mother and also kissed her hand with a nod.

"Ah, Mr. Reyas—you are so new here, but at last a gentlemen has come to our house." The matronly woman, whose name was Valorie, took the crook of his arm and led him into the dining room to show him a place beside her at the great table set in fine china and sparkling glassware.

He put her chair in behind her as the boy had instructed, waiting until Felicia was settled across from him and then he nodded to his host. They took their places. He swept the napkin into his lap and then wondered what he must do next—*madre de Dios,* so much for him to remember.

"Father says you are looking to buy a ranch," Felicia offered.

"Yes, you know of any for sale?"

She dropped her gaze and shook her head. He felt abandoned for the moment. He had missed his cue on what to say to her. Damn, the boy and him had practiced this so many times. He must speak of light things, not of business, nor sickness, nor death—what the hell were they to speak about?

"How large a ranch do you wish to purchase?" Valorie asked, passing him a plate with meat that the father had carved from a great beef roast.

"Big enough to run a large horse herd and some cattle."

"Perhaps up on the Gila above town?"

He set the plate down and agreed. Unfamiliar with that country, he could only say yes.

"Do you know of any ranches for sale?" he asked, looking from the mother to the daughter.

"I suspect there are several. The dry weather has discouraged many of the big ones owned by absentee owners," Valorie said.

"I would appreciate any advice you have."

"Perhaps the Cross R," her husband said, taking potatoes from the bowl and passing them toward her.

He knew all about those white ones, though he much preferred yams, which they called sweet potatoes. So when he placed some on his plate, he offered the bowl to Felicia, but she had them. Green beans were next and he took some, then came some soda biscuits and he also placed one on his plate.

"The Cross R is for sale?" he asked.

"Oh yes, the man who owns it had an unfortunate accident in El Paso," her father said.

Reyas frowned and then realized that Felicia had caught him at it when she spoke. "What Father means, he was shot in a card game in El Paso for cheating."

He thanked her, but he also noticed the look of disapproval on the man's face. Still, the smallest of confident grins remained on her face as she went about her food. He felt he had scored something with her. The boy had warned him, it would be slow, she was not some cantina *puta*.

So the meal went smoothly enough, save for the knots in

his stomach, and after they finished he and the father went out on the porch to smoke cigars.

"Ramon says you are interested in investments?" The man blew smoke away and sat back in the wicker chair.

"*Si*—yes. He says you have some interesting plans."

"Freight our own up here from the railhead at Demming. A new store in Alma perhaps too."

"How many wagons would we need?"

"Four to start."

"Mules or oxen?"

"I think with mules you make faster time."

"Oh yes," Reyas agreed, listening to the cicadas begin their evening hissing. "I will send him over tomorrow and you two can figure the deal. He is much better on figures than I am."

"Very good." The man extended a hand and shook his hand. "We have a deal?"

"Yes," he said and stood. Never did he get a drag from the cigar.

"We best put these out and save them. The dessert is ready."

"Oh yes, dessert," he said and wondered if he would throw up if he ate any more of their strange food. Beef, sheep, frijoles and tortillas were enough for anyone—but not for these gringos.

So his partnership began and the McCain-Reyas Freight lines began with four wagons and twenty good mules. After several meals at the house, he finally asked Felicia if she might picnic with him the next Saturday. With her parents' approval, he prepared for the journey. A gentle, high-stepping, buggy mare was chosen and the rig with leather seats and a collapsible top as well as lights for night driving was purchased.

The boy showed him "the secluded place" on a test drive to where some rustling cottonwoods shaded a grassy glen fed by a small stream, a reasonable drive from her house. Then the boy explained the proper way to picnic, how to spread the blanket on the ground and put out the things, allowing her to take charge of it. Then to speak of his "dreams" when she asked.

The Saturday came and he picked her up. With polite nods and words to her mother, he assured Valorie that her daughter would be back before supper. So with her beside him, they began the journey at a gentle pace, nodding to people passing by them on horseback and buckboard. They were a swarthy-skinned gringo businessman and his pale-skinned girlfriend in the blue dress, who sat so stiff-backed and proper at his side he wondered if she even understood the ways of men and women.

They reached the spot and he mannerly helped her down, then, carrying the blanket and basket, followed her to the edge of the deep shade. She removed the bonnet to let the wind sweep her face and curled hair.

"This is a heavenly place, señor."

He nodded and spread the blanket, then bowed when it and the basket were in the proper place. He felt ready to bust, but tried to remain calm. Their plan needed to work—so far so good.

"My, you are such a gentleman." She took her place very demurely on the opposite side of the basket. Her feet tucked underneath the dress, she fanned herself absently with the bonnet. "In fact, I have never known a person so polite in all my life."

"Nor have I known a woman of your beauty," he said and smiled.

She looked skyward and blushed. "And you are way too generous with your comments, sir."

"No, I am an honest man."

"I must say you make me want to swoon."

"Here," he said and poured her a glass of red wine in the fine long-stemmed crystal glass. What did swoon mean anyway?

She rose on her knees and admired the sun sparkling on the glassware. "My, but this is expensive."

"Nothing but the best for you, my dear."

"Wonderful," she said and downed the glass's contents with an "ah."

He refilled her glass again and sipped on his own. Four or five glasses later, she was dancing a ballet across the meadow and challenging him to remove his tie and coat and enjoy the freedom. She sang songs as she pranced about. He followed her with the ready bottle. Her skirt was raised to show her snowy ankles and part of her legs when she splashed barefoot in the small stream like a free person.

On the bank, she held the back of her hand to her forehead and looked ready to faint. He set down the wine and caught her in his arms in time to swoop her up. In his arms, she felt featherlight and looked at him from half-opened eyes.

"You are so polite, I know you won't take advantage of me."

He kissed her, holding her in his arms. She put her arms loosely around his neck and giggled. "Do that again."

When he rose his head up from kissing her on the mouth, her eyes looked even more glossy. "Wow, that was something—you—wow."

He gently laid her on the blanket and kissed her softly, while his hands drew up her dress, feeling the silkiness of her legs. Then he undid the buttons on the front of her dress, brushing his lips across hers as he drew up the silk cover and exposed the small, stone-hard breasts with large, turgid nipples. His mouth closed over one and she screamed. Then she clutched him to them as he sucked on the right one while he undid her bloomer buttons. He swept them off her legs and soon ran his palm between her legs. She raised her knees, swaying them from side to side as he sought her with his finger.

At last consumed with desire, he rose up and ripped off his belt and the buttons on the fly, shoving his pants down, and he soon held his turgid dick in his hand. Sorting her weaving knees, he came between them and started his aching member into her.

Her scream drew a smile. It will not hurt long, my virgin lover, he silently promised her. Then he began to work his way into the untouched walls, punching his route deeper and deeper, savoring the first-time pleasures of the unopened vault. He lifted her legs to spread them and went further with the force in his butt wanting all of the way inside her. His breath raged and soon he knew his time was about to arrive—when he started to come, he looked down underneath him and discovered she had fainted—he let loose and drove himself to the bottom of her well.

On his knees, he whispered in her ear. "Wake up, my angel."

She blinked and tried to shove him back. "What happened to me?" Then as she sat up, her lower jaw dropped and she pointed at his dick in shocked horror.

"You didn't!" She looked aghast at him.

He sat back on his heels, considering she might need it again. "We made love."

"No! No! You have raped me!"

"You don't understand—" He reached for her, but she sat up and began to strike at him. Her face went pale. She choked and then began to vomit. Despite his effort to get back, the hot rush from her mouth went on his shirt and the rest covered his privates as she heaved up more and more. He managed to shed his pants, and shaking his head, looked at the mess on his clothing with the south wind sweeping his bare legs. Aw, damn her!

Washing the mess off in the creek, he left his shirt to dry on a bush and went back to the blanket were she lay passed out. Surprised when he rolled her out of the fetal position, her dress looked unscathed. The small hard-rock breasts still pointed skyward and the dried blood on the inside of her legs was the only sign of their transgressions. By then he had a new hard-on and again he stuck it into her with her moaning the whole time he was hurting her.

With a cold towel to her face and several trips to the creek, he sobered her up and managed to rearrange her dress and clothes.

"What are you going to do to me next?" she slurred as he carried her in his arms to the buggy.

"Marry you."

"Marry me? You can't do that."

He looked at the sun low in the west. He needed to hurry; the boy and his surprise for her would be waiting for him. "Yes, you will be my wife before long."

"I don't want to be your wife." She began to sob.

"Why not? You already have my son in your belly."

She looked shaken and clutched her stomach and glanced down to see. "That's what you did to me?"

"Yes and someday you will beg me to do it to you all the time."

"Never. It was despicable."

He reached over and patted her stomach. "You'll look cute with that belly full of my son."

"You—!" She screamed and began to pummel him with the sides of her fists.

He shed them like stray raindrops and made the mare hurry. Soon he saw the boy and the man in the black frock coat on horseback waiting in the road. He reined up and the preacher rode in close, and he began to read from his book.

She began to protest and Reyas closed his hand over her mouth, giving the answers for both of them as the mild-mannered, bearded preacher continued the service unfettered by her struggle as Reyas contained her with both hands.

"—I hereby pronounce you man and wife. Good day, Mrs. Reyas, and you, sir." He tipped his hat, turned his skinny horse and accepted the money for the license from the boy.

"How could he do that?" she asked, slumped in the seat, pale as a ghost.

"We simply told him you had gotten pregnant by a murderer who was about to hang and I offered to marry you to save you the shame of bastardhood."

She drew a deep breath up her nose. "And now what?"

"We will tell your parents we eloped today."

"They won't believe that."

"They will if you say so. You don't want them dead, do you?"

"You would kill them?" Her blue eyes flew wide open in disbelief.

"If they try to take you from me."

Defeated, she shook her head and turned the other way from him. He clucked to the mare and they headed for town. All the way he whistled the song of the wild *caballo*.

25

When they crossed by the pyramid border marker, Slocum wondered if they could reach Demming by dark. It was still a good ride ahead and their animals were weakening from the long way with little more than short rations of grain for sustenance.

Long past midnight they reached the railhead. At the Carson Livery and wagon yard, they watered the animals and rubbed them down while Magdellania went to find them some food. The horses and mules were eating on two five-dollar-a-bale Missouri timothy hay when she returned with a sack full of tamales and three bottles of red wine.

They feasted on the food and drink. The old hustler joined them, smoking a corncob pipe that was filled with aromatic tobacco.

"Guess them teamsters from McCain and Reyas ain't coming in tonight."

"You say Reyas, señor?" she asked.

"Yeah, he's some rich Messikin moved into Silver City, joined up with that Howard McCain and got them a freight line going to haul stuff up there."

"How recently?" Slocum asked, seated on the ground with his knees drawn up as he ate another tamale.

"Started freighting last week. Some guy came through here asking about that Reyas, oh, a couple of weeks or so ago. Never seen him again either. Said he worked for this Reyas in Messico."

"What did he look like?" Slocum asked.

"Like a toad, ugly as hell, kinda squat."

"Torga," she said.

The old man shook his head. "Never got his name."

"He got away from the Ruralists," Bronco said. "In all the confusion."

Slocum nodded—someone else to watch for when they arrived there. "This Reyas must be pretty rich?"

The old man made a sharp nod. "Figure he financed the four double wagons and all them mules to tug them up there. They ain't trash either."

"What will we do?" Cyd asked, looking concerned.

"We've got only our business to handle," he said to silence the boy and not let Old Whiskers know too much about their venture.

"You boys looking for this Reyas too?"

Slocum shook his head. "These boys only knew him from Mexico. We better shake out some bedrolls and get some sleep; tomorrow we've still got a ways to go."

She nodded, but he didn't miss the grim set to her mouth in the dim lantern light. He wanted to reach over and hug away any of her fears, but it wasn't the place. She rolled out her blanket and the others followed. The rooster would crow soon enough.

He did too. From some corral fence, the red cockerel heralded the sun's first flannel light. Eyes still dry and mouth the same, they staggered out and washed their faces in the horse trough. Some sort of clarity came to Slocum's eyes. It was the sight of Magdellania's shapely butt swinging past that made him want to grin. Good enough. Silver City lay north. Preparing the pads, saddles and then the packs, they had about completed the chore when she hurriedly returned with a sack of burritos and more wine.

They mounted up and ate as they rode across the Southern Pacific track, heading up the sandy road for the distant line of mountains. A long-eared jackrabbit looked them over before he bounded off into the dry bunch grass and greasewood. Overhead, a lazy buzzard sought the updraft to stay afloat looking for carrion.

The past day's heat evaporated, the gusts of wind felt cool enough to make her wrap herself in a blanket shawl. On the eastern horizon, the sun tried to climb over it and promised another cloudless day.

"It is a long ways up here?" Bronco said, weary-looking from their days in the saddle.

"Not close, perhaps forty miles," Slocum said.

"I figured that the worst enemy is not the bandits," Cyd said from in the back.

"They can be there too," he said, over his shoulder.

"My butt is sure telling me it's a long way," Bronco said and stood in the stirrups. "Outlaws, dry water holes, no feed, it sure won't be no easy job getting a pack train up here."

"You catch sight of them pretty señoritas up there, you'll think it was a hop and jump up here," Slocum teased them.

"They got some up there?"

"Them back in Demming looked ugly to me," Cyd said. "I seen two or three of them—whew."

"Railroaders ain't particular," Slocum said and then he laughed at her frown of disapproval.

Midday, they spotted a flock of buzzards circling and Slocum told them to stay back and short loped the roan ahead. He could see why the freight wagons never made it the night before. One rig was on its side, dead mules all over and the bodies of men scattered where they'd been back shot. Lots of goods were scattered across the ground. The only sounds were the flap of the buzzards taking wing and others fighting over the tender parts of the bloodiest mules.

"Who did this?" She reined her chestnut in the circle of destruction.

"Whoever wanted the silver bullion, I figure."

"That it?"

"Strongboxes broken open over there and the bars were loaded on pack animals. Used some of the freight lines mules to pack them too."

"What can we do?" she asked.

"Bronco, you ride back and tell the Demming sheriff about this, then come on to Silver City. Just avoid Reyas and that Torga. You'll find us."

"What can I do?" Cyd asked, dismounting as Bronco sent his mule off racing to the south.

"We better cover up these bodies with canvas till the law gets here."

"Cut it off the wagon tops?" she asked.

"Yes." He climbed up on a wheel and used his knife to strip off the ropes holding on the sheeting. In a short time, they had the corpses under cover and the buzzards had three dead mules to breakfast upon. Satisfied, Slocum started to remount when he noticed a glitter. Stepping down, he picked up a diamond stick pin and admired it as he remounted. None of the hardcase freighters had ever owned such a piece of jewelry. No, this was lost by someone else—one of the robbers? He wondered and pocketed it. The three rode north with their mules, with nothing more they could do for the dead.

Past sundown in Silver City, they found Helm's Wagon Yard and put their animals in the tie stalls.

"You saying they massacred them wagons?" the excited livery man asked.

Slocum nodded in the dim lantern light. He and Cyd used wads of grass hay to rub down their animals. The horses' teeth chomped on the hard corn as they worked to make the exhausted animals more comfortable.

"Who knows about this robbery?" a loud voice demanded coming in the lighted hallway. The big man introduced himself as the sheriff.

"I sent word to the law down here," Slocum said, squatted on his boot heels. Eating sliced beef sandwiches she brought

back from a cafe for them, he looked up at the bowlegged
lawman before he went on to explain.

"Must have jumped them about dark north of Demming.
Every man was dead. Shot in the back. I've got half a han-
kering they knew the robbers. They turned over one wagon,
but it was still when they rolled it over. Shot two mules, but
they weren't in harness."

"You saw a helluva lot." The lawman frowned.

Slocum looked up at him. "All the signs were there on the
ground. They used part of the mules to pack it off with."

"Pack it?"

"Silver bullion, I figure. The strongboxes were all busted
open and empty."

The sheriff shook his head. "No, those were carrying gold.
Get some out of all that smelting. Saved it up to make a
shipment to the mint."

Slocum nodded. That made a lot of difference. Silver bullion wasn't easy to sell, but gold was universal.

"You said you figured they knew the robbers?" the sheriff
asked.

"The men weren't in their wagons, had no weapons out.
All were shot like they were running away, what weren't
shot up close. Rifles in their wagons. What do you think?"

"I don't know what to think. Any other clues?"

"Maybe." Slocum rose and took the stick pin out of his
pocket. "Seen this before?"

The man bent over to examine it in his palm and then
looked out the top of his eyes at him. "Only man owns one
of them that big is a banker here in town by the name of
Cartwright."

"He here?"

"Nope, he went to Sante Fe yesterday on banking business."

"He could have lost it." Slocum closed his hand and pocketed it.

"Could have. What's your name?"

"Slocum."

"You here on business I guess?"

"Yes. Setting up a smelting deal for a mine in Mexico."

"Stay around a few days, I may have more questions for you about that robbery and that pin."

"A few days and I need to get back."

"A few is enough. Have you talked to Reyas or McCain?"

"Didn't plan to."

"Guess that's your business."

"I sent a man back to Demming to tell the sheriff there. We covered the bodies for them to look at and so the buzzards couldn't eat them."

"You did your share." Then the man shook his head warily. "I've had more trouble the past six weeks than we've had in years around here. Some boy from Mexico got himself killed somehow—no marks. Got two more hung after that, another packer shot himself, and some drunk Messikin drown in six inches of water."

"Who was the boy?" Slocum asked, sharing a concerned look with her.

"Alphanso—"

"The bookkeeper—" she gasped.

"Pardon me, ma'am?"

"Reyas's bookkeeper was Alphanso," Slocum explained.

"His bookkeeper, I figured that. Could have been poisoned or smothered, no way to know, except excuse me, ma'am, he had no clothes on. Reyas bought him some for the burial."

"Who was the packer?" Slocum asked.

"Hernandos something."

"He came from the valley too," she said.

"Who was the Mexican that drowned?" Slocum asked.

"No name, short, squat, real ugly, looked like a big toad."

"Torga?" she asked, her eyes wide in shock at the discovery.

"What the hell they all have to do with each other?" the lawman demanded.

"All these people you mentioned came from the valley in the mountains in Mexico where Reyas ran the mine like some kind of king. One day there was revolution and he fled," Slocum explained.

"I'd sure need proof he did these murders. But it makes sense. Still, he can hire him one of them fancy lawyers out of Sante Fe and blow my poor prosecutor away. I'd need real hard proof."

"Sorry, we have none," Slocum said with a shrug.

"I'll do some more checking. Oh, I won't mention your name around Reyas—but don't kill him in my county, please."

"Try not to," Slocum said.

"Damn, oh damn—" The sheriff left the barn, shaking his head ruefully.

"Shall we sleep here?" she asked.

Slocum shook his head; he had a better idea. "Cyd can watch our things and wait for Bronco. Early in the morning we will meet you," he said to Cyd and herded her out of the alleyway.

They started up the boardwalk.

"Where are we going?" she asked under her breath.

"To sleep in a real bed in a hotel with you."

She caught his arm in both hands and pressed her forehead to his shoulder. "Ah, good."

He didn't want to tell her this might be their last night together, civilization usually messed up a lot of things for him. Somehow he had a feeling things were closing in on him—they still needed a bookkeeper and a smelting agreement for the mine.

Sunup began to flannel the eastern sky. Dressed, Slocum and Magdellania hurried for the stables and both men were ready, looking fresher, Slocum felt certain, than the two of them felt. But he had earned the catch in his back from the night before and the little sleep they found could hardly be blamed on much more than strong desires for each other's bodies. Whew, he wished his head would clear, so he could think.

"How will we find this bookkeeper?" she asked as they marched up the boardwalk in the shadowy first light for a cafe.

"There will be one, trust me."

"I do, but—"

He nodded and they entered the cafe. A large, buxom Mexican woman waited on them.

"Good morning," she said, looking them over.

"We need four breakfasts," he said to her.

Cyd and Bronco jerked off their dusty sombreros and she gave them a serious look over. "*Huevos ranchos* good enough?"

"*Muy bueno,*" Bronco said and she smiled at the two again, who quickly nodded.

She went off singing and the two men about laughed aloud, quickly taking their place at the table.

In minutes, she returned with mugs of steaming coffee. She looked over them to see who could hear what she said as she placed them on the table.

"You have any money in the bank?" she asked in a low voice.

Slocum shook his head.

"Good, they say it's failed. It'll hurt lots of people here."

"All the money is gone?" Slocum asked.

"Yes, they say the banker absconded with what was left." She blinked her large brown eyes.

"His name is Cartwright," Slocum asked, recalling the paper in his pocket. That might mean that Reyas lost his fortune too.

"You knew him?" she asked.

"Yes, I'd heard of him," Slocum said. "Do you know of a bookkeeper that can be hired? We need one for our mine."

She folded her arms over her ample breasts. "Yes, there is an American down the street. His name is McBroom. He use to work for the Sierra Mining Company, but the ore petered out."

"McBroom?"

"Douglas McBroom."

"Married?"

"No, why?"

"The mine is deep in Mexico. A married man might not want to take his family there."

"Hey, good morning," she said to some new customers coming in the doorway.

Slocum thanked her and nodded in approval to Magdellania. "He would know lots about the business."

She agreed and soon the buxom waitress delivered the large plates of eggs, chili peppers, pork, potatoes and a steaming stack of flour tortillas. The rich smells alone made Slocum's empty stomach churn in anticipation. This was a good place to eat.

An hour later, the foursome sat in the small office. Douglas McBroom removed his gold-rimmed glasses and set them down on the ledger. A slender man, clean shaven, his blue eyes looked clear despite the fact he had taken off the reading glasses. Slocum guessed him to be thirty.

After introductions, Slocum explained their purpose and openly asked the man if he would consider taking such a post.

"Mexico, huh?"

"Yes. Deep in the Sierra Madras. This is a rich mine. The ore's rich enough to ship up here by burro train for smelting."

"Be a challenge," he said.

"How much did you do at the Sierra mine?" Slocum asked. He also noticed the man was having a hard time not looking at Magdellania. Not offensively, more fascination, he guessed.

"I bought the supplies, dynamite, drills, mine track, everything and kept the books."

"This place is so remote you can't get iron tracks in there."

"Who owns it?"

"The people who work it."

McBroom nodded. "Salary?"

"If you are as good as you say you are, two hundred a month."

The man tried to act calm. It was obvious from his small office and the lack of fixtures that amount far exceeded his monthly income in Silver City. The quiet grew deeper.

"Of course, we would expect you to help us make the smelter agreement too."

McBroom nodded.

"Señor," she spoke up. "You would have a fine casa to live in and a cook to keep your house."

"Man would be a damn fool to turn all that down." He smiled at her and nodded quickly.

Slocum stuck out his hand and they shook. Then the two men who Slocum decided understood little of their talks in English shook the man's hand too. At last, McBroom shook her hand and looked a fraction too long into her eyes.

The smelter deal with McBroom along came off smooth and Slocum recognized the man's knowledge of the business. He felt they had hired the right man. They rode back to Silver City and dismounted at the cafe to go in and eat their supper. Magdellania was busy translating to the pair of men all about the deal made at the smelter.

"I may need you to help me translate at the mine," McBroom said to her. "My Spanish is very rusty."

She swept past him going inside and nodded. "I can help."

"Good."

At the cafe's doorway, from the corner of his eye, Slocum spotted a blanket-rumped Appaloosa horse and a familiar-looking rider going past in the street with another horse and rider beside him. The deep black circles in the snow-white blanket on the Ap made him quickly turn away. The Abbott brothers were in Silver City. *Damn!* Those two bounty hunters from Ft. Scott, Kansas, had arrived. Their expenses were paid by a rich man whose son had been killed in a gunfight; the two Kansas deputy sheriffs were the bane of Slocum's life.

"Cyd, take my roan horse out back in the alley for me," he said, under his breath.

The man paused for a second then turned on his heel and hurried to obey. Slocum shook his head at Magdellania to silence her protest.

"Take McBroom back to the mine for me," he said to her in a soft tone. "I have no time to explain." Then he looked over at McBroom. "She can get you to the mine, do your translations and help you get settled. Nice to meet you. Magdellania take care of these men. See they get back and that the mine works for all the people."

He handed her the money purse. "You are in charge."

She blinked her eyes, then nodded. "We are grateful."

"Cyd will be waiting." He winked at her, then headed out through the kitchen, getting surprised looks from the culinary help.

In the alley he swung in the saddle, thanked Cyd and set the blue roan on his way.

"Vaya con Dios!" Cyd shouted after him.

God better be with him. He had no one else, Slocum decided as he crossed the street and proceeded on the blue roan into the next litter-strewed alleyway.

26

The dusty town of Lordsburg sat upon the greasewood flats along the iron rails of the Southern Pacific tracks. A smattering of adobe and weathered-board, false-front saloons and stores were surrounded by jackals. Bare-assed, brown-skinned children in ragged tops stopped in a line to stare at his passing. Grubby hands managed to sweep the unkept hair back from their faces because of the wind. Their privates were exposed until puberty when they would need to be covered by pants or skirts. The youngsters soon returned to their noisy play.

He stopped at a weathered hovel. The plaster cracked and a lot of the exposed adobe bricks on the corners were worn round by the elements. A woman came to the door, whipped the long hair back from her face and twisted it on her shoulder.

"Slocum," she said in recognition and her full lips formed a smile.

"Buster around?" he asked, seeing the small corral was empty.

She shook her head. "He's gone to Tucson."

"Business?"

She shrugged and he wondered if he had asked the wrong question.

"Some men shot his brother—" She dropped her gaze to the ground.

"He's gone to find them."

She nodded, then her eyes grew very concerned. "You must know that she has her *pistoleros* out looking for you."

He looked off to the hills in the south. "I've heard that."

"They say she wants your head."

"She's not alone. Can I buy a meal?"

"Oh, how ungracious of me. Come in. The wind is bad today, so I must cook in here. I have some beans and some tortillas."

"That will be enough."

"Where will you go?" she asked over her shoulder.

"I better go to her ranch."

She whirled around. "She'll kill you—"

He shrugged. "Two bounty hunters rode into Silver City looking for me yesterday."

"But she—"

He nodded and squatted on his boot heels on the dirt floor. Aside from the pallet of blankets on the floor, the hovel contained little else, but a small sheet-iron stove and a rusty pipe that went out through the roof. Her and Buster had very little and with him off looking for his brother's killers, he had obviously not provided much of anything for her in his absence.

He ate her food in silence. Grateful for the nourishment, he tried to think how to help her. Masticating the spicy, soft beans he knew he must leave her some money—Buster should have taken her along. But he might have been broke too at the time he left, as there was not a lot of work for the ex–civilian mule packers that had kept the army supplied during the Apache campaign in Mexico.

She sat upon the blankets, cross-legged, the skirt covering her legs and feet. Some of her youthful beauty, he recalled, edged by the more serious look on her face and the rounding of her body made her more attractive than the slender girl he first met a decade before.

"No children?"

She shook her head.

"Buster will be back," he promised, not looking at her.

"If I had had his children he would come back."

"No," he dismissed her words. "He never said he wouldn't be back, did he?"

"No, he said, like always, see you soon."

"He will." Finished, he drank from the gourd she dipped out of the *oyyah* for him.

On his feet, he dug out a double eagle and pressed it in her hand. "Here, buy some food and material. You will need a new dress for when he comes back."

"You will need this," she said, looking at the coin in shock.

He hugged her shoulders and kissed her cheek. "I owed Buster that for years."

"No . . ."

Outside in the whistling wind, he tightened the cinch. Then he swung his leg over the blue roan and waved good-bye. He could see the tears running down her dark cheeks as she waved good-bye at him.

Headed west, he jogged the roan. His plans were to take the San Pedro Valley south across the border. If he went back to Mexico like he came out, chances were good those two would be on his tracks. Heading west, by late afternoon he watched the sun sink low over the faroff Chiricahuas and the range before them.

By sundown, he reached a small railroad town with a switch. The only cantina looked small. He hitched the roan at the rack and went inside. Several of the track hands were in the bar and looked at him mildly as they hoisted their beer mugs.

"Can I get any food?" he asked the whiskered bartender.

"Stew's all."

Slocum nodded and looked around. The railroad crowd acted friendly enough. The man brought back a bowl floating with some cooked meat and stewed tomatoes. He found a spoon under the counter, looked at it and wiped it on the side of his pants before he set it down beside the bowl.

"Anything to drink?"

"Beer'll be fine."

27

"What do you mean they robbed and killed—" Reyas felt a sharp pain in his chest that forced him to jam his fist against his breastplate to stem the hurting. A knife stabbed him in the heart at the news. Bandits killed everyone on the freight train, took the mules and the gold—his breath grew shorter.

"You all right?" the boy demanded.

"Just—shocked—" He collapsed on a chair. Unable to breathe, he grew fainter, dizzier-headed and then passed out.

He awoke. Dazed and shaken, he looked into the pale face of his sweet wife busy washing his face with a damp cloth.

"You all right?" she asked.

"Tell me more about the robbery," he managed in such a husky voice that it even shocked him.

"We only know what we have heard."

"What's that?"

"Not much but what we first heard." She wrung out the rag in a bowl on the stand beside the bed.

What wasn't she telling him? He knew something else was wrong by her look. "Where is Ramon now?"

"Ramon has gone to the bank to check on things there."

"What is wrong there?"

"Someone came by and told him the bank has failed and the doors were locked."

"Failed?" He frowned at her, not able to comprehend her words.

She swallowed to get up her courage, then spoke softly. "They say that Cartwright has taken all the money and run away."

"When did this happen?"

"A man—" She shook her head. "I don't know him—he came by and told Ramon that while you were unconscious. Ramon went to see what he could do about your money."

"You mean all my money is gone too—" He started to rise, but a new wave of helplessness spread over him. Slumped back, he wondered what ailed him. Like someone had pulled the plug out of him. Never in his life had he ever felt so weak.

"You must be still. The doctor is supposed to come soon," she said, wringing her small hands.

"I don't need—no doctor."

"Yes, you do," she said.

Her words struck him like a bullwhip. She thought—she knew something about his condition—the reason why he was so drained and she wouldn't tell him, he felt certain. If only he could get more air; he tore loose the kerchief from around his neck and then lay back. Still not enough air came. He had not ran anywhere. Why was he so out of breath?

To escape, he closed his eyes and soon sleep took him to a tormented hell. Apaches sought him. He tried to hide from them. He was forced to crawl through spiny beds of cactus and, bare-handed, he had to strangle diamondback rattlers. Their rattles shook like thunder and clapped so loud they hurt his ears. Everywhere spiny points jabbed at him.

Mad war cries in his head, he awoke in a cold, clammy sweat that soaked his clothing. The reflection in the gringo's glasses told him how wide-eyed and pale he really looked, then the man put a silver piece on his chest and listened with things stuck in his ears.

"Breathe," he said and still listened. At last, the doctor straightened and looked aside for his wife.

"Is he Catholic?"

"I'm not certain," she said. "What's wrong?"

"Bad as his heart sounds, he won't live long. If you want to fetch a priest, I'll stay here with him."

"No priest," he managed to gasp. "I have no love for them."

"But—" she protested. "Oh, what will I do?"

"Don't worry about me—" He ran out of breath, and the pain grew sharper in his chest. Her small hands squeezed his right one and he forced a smile to reassure her.

"He don't want a priest, there is little more I can do for him," the doctor said and started to put on his coat.

"No medicine that you can give him?" she asked.

The physician shook his head. "His heart is gone. Probably exploded. I can't heal what is broken internally."

"How long will he live?"

The man lowered his voice, but Reyas heard him say, "—before daylight in the morning."

She caught a scream and covered her mouth with her hand.

"Sorry, Mrs. Reyas. God be with you," the doctor said to him and turned to leave.

No! Reyas tried to scream after him that he lied, but no words came from his mouth. His jaw would not even open. How long had he lain there in one place on the bed? It was like he'd become frozen in place since the doctor left him with that death sentence.

Unable to even talk, he tried to shout—he wasn't dying. Wrong. He was only resting until he could get his strength back. No words came out nor did his jaw want to hinge. Precious little air came through his nose and he desperately wanted more. Like he was being smothered to death under a pillow.

Soon she came to kneel at the edge of the bed and began to pray for him. He wanted to smile at her sincerity. Even the muscles in his face refused to respond, so he looked at the tin ceiling tiles and wished she knew he was still alive and could hear the words he wanted to say to her.

Hours passed and his situation did not improve. She lighted a small lamp and resumed her vigil. He began to feel that by morning he would be improved and able to tell her something. Then Ramon returned.

"What did you learn about the bank?" she asked, standing up to speak to him.

"—bad news. Cartwright took all the money out of the safe and a fast horse out of here. I fear your husband has lost thousands."

"What will we do?" she asked, sounding so lonely.

Reyas wished for his voice so hard—but nothing came out.

"What does the doctor say about him?" Ramon asked, motioning to Reyas.

"That he won't live to see the sunrise."

Ramon waved his hands over Reyas's face, then leaned over and peered into his eyes. "Is he dead now?"

Reyas could see her hug the boy's arm and fear-filled, she looked over at him. "He hasn't spoke except to say for me not to get the priest."

"I think he's dead now."

"What should we do—get the undertaker?"

"No," he said and twisted her around to face him. Then his fingers began to unto the buttons on the front of her dress. "We can celebrate."

"But—" Her fingers captured his.

He bent over and kissed her. Her hands went around his neck—they were no strangers to each other. In no time, he pushed the dress off her bare shoulders. In the flickering lamplight, Reyas could see him fondling her small breasts as they kissed. A new fury rushed like a volcano in his chest as the boy stripped away the clothing from her slender body.

She undid his belt with a hard jerk. Soon from the corner of his eye, he could see the boy's erection waving about like a flag pole as she hurriedly undressed him. Then they disappeared from his vision, but he could hear them on the floor scrambling about. Ramon's grunting lanced Reyas's guts— her cries of pleasure only made him more anxious, angrier and ready to jump from the bed and kill both of them. Then things began to fade.

"What will we do for money?" Reyas listened to his wife's words. Unable to speak out and curse their betrayal of him, he fought to stay awake.

"You're still a very rich woman. He has secured thousands of dollars here at the house. There are those fancy stallions of his at Cartwright's to sell and the proceeds from the last two pack trains. You're rich!"

"No, Ramon," she said very strongly. "I will be the sad widow for a few months, then you will marry me and we will both be rich."

He watched them from the corner of his eyes. Two naked bodies hugging and dancing around the room in celebration. His vision narrowed until all he could see were their bare behinds spinning past him. Them having all the damn fun and pleasure at his expense. . . .

28

Slocum sat for long while on the roan horse and studied the familiar hacienda's layout. Obviously the ranch hands were gone. A few of the domestics went about their usual chores, drawing water, tending the chickens, goats, working the garden plot. Satisfied there was little security to oppose him down there, he booted the roan off the hillside and rode through the yucca and scattered mesquite toward the sprawling headquarters.

Overhead, a few buzzard scouts circled on the updraft. Looking for a possible meal on some refuse or guts from butchering dumped aside that the cur dogs would fight them over.

Soon these guardians of the hacienda began to acknowledge his approach with their cowardly yaps from the safety of beneath carts or with a ready way to retreat from a free boot kick. A buxom woman came out on the porch, shaded her eyes with her hands and stared hard in his direction.

"Mother of God!" she shouted. "It's him!" And she disappeared inside the house, screaming at the top of her lungs, "He's come back! He's come back!"

He wet his cracked lower lip and booted the hesitant roan

out of the brush and onto the open bare dirt space that surrounded the casa. Soon a familiar figure appeared with both hands defiantly on her hips. He rode within twenty feet of her. Close enough to read the fire dancing in the pools of brown eyes, to see the quiver in her full lower lip. Then he threw his leg over and dismounted. With slow, deliberate efforts, he loosened the latigo leathers of the cinch, ignoring the imposing figure on the porch.

With a scream escaping her throat, the quirt held high, she charged off the porch. "You bastard! How dare you?"

He caught her whip hand and wrenched the quirt off her wrist so hard she grasped for her arm in pain. Then he jerked her up close and glared into her eyes.

"I'm going to give you what your father should have given you when you were a little girl," he said.

She wilted, taken aback. But her fear was short-lived as he herded her to the porch. With newfound vigor, she began to try to kick and hit at him. All to no avail, for he held her squirming form around the waist with one arm and undid the ties of her skirt with the other hand. He stripped down the skirt and the silken underwear to expose her bare backside. Taking a seat on the edge of the porch with her bent over his lap, he began to spank the olive-colored half-moons of her butt with his hand.

Her cries of, "Oh, no!" echoed off the hills. With each resounding whack of his hand, her defiance grew dimmer and soon she began to cry.

"Please? Please? No more, I promise—" she begged.

At last, he set her up and glared hard into her wet lashes. "Promise me you will never use that quirt on anything again, man or beast."

"—I—I, ah, promise—" Her body was racked with sobs as he held her by both arms.

"You ever do it again—" He waited for her reply.

"I won't. I won't." The tears ran in rivers down her smooth complexion.

"Ever—"

"Ever, I promise." The she buried her face into his shoulder. "Why did you leave me?"

"Because you are too spoiled to stand at times."

"I will never be that again." She drew her head back and used her hands to thread the long, copper-tinted black hair back from her face. "How long can you stay this time?"

He looked past her at the yucca-studded hills. "As long as they let me and you behave."

She hugged him and laid her face on his vest. "Good, you can stay here for a long time."

He nodded, but in his heart he knew better. In a sweep, he gathered her in his arms. She kicked free of the skirt tangled around her feet as he stood.

"What will the servants think?" she asked.

"Whatever they want to think."

Her free laughter carried across the chaparral. With the mixture of the desert's creosote perfume and her sweet musk in his nostrils, he felt heady carrying her through the open doorway.

That they stayed off his trail for a while was all he asked.

Watch for

SLOCUM AT DEVIL'S MOUTH

289th novel in the exciting SLOCUM series
from Jove

Coming in March!